"HERE THERE ARE DRAGONS" . . .

. . . had been the last message from the starship *Ar-numatek,* transmitted seconds before the starship veered into the Antilian sun. Now, a generation later, the *Skip-jack* retraced the earlier vessel's course, its fate uncertain; an alien being called *Elluvon* lay wounded in the ship's sick bay, its mission unknown; and an Elluvon armada approached from a great distance, its might greater than any the *Skipjack*'s captain, Paul Riker, had ever seen. And as the *Skipjack* approached the point where legend placed the dragons' mating ground, Captain Riker knew that he and his crew were already involved in a mission of greater peril than any they had ever faced!

Simon Lang

The Elluvon Gift

AVON
PUBLISHERS OF BARD, CAMELOT, DISCUS, EQUINOX AND FLARE BOOKS

THE ELLUVON GIFT is an original publication of
Avon Books.

AVON BOOKS
A division of
The Hearst Corporation
959 Eighth Avenue
New York, New York 10019

First Avon Printing, October, 1975

AVON TRADEMARK REG. U.S. PAT. OFF. AND
FOREIGN COUNTRIES, REGISTERED TRADEMARK—
MARCA REGISTRADA, HECHO EN CHICAGO, U.S.A.

Printed in the U.S.A.

To my best friend, Al Hartman,
who has been down the tubes
with me many times—and out
again.

The Elluvon Gift

Prolog

It was the day for celebrating life.

It was a day for praising death.

The day of the ceremony fell, with conspicuous premeditation, upon the Feast of the Unborn Martyrs, with a grateful nod to the U.S.S. *Skipjack*, the federation ship that had snatched the last remnant of a dying race—sixty fertilized eggs—from the searing maw of a nova. In that spectacular show of heroism, only a handful of crewmen had lost their lives, and only one woman.

Now, in the presence of the Secretary General, various ambassadors, delegates, and emissaries from half a dozen star systems, religious dignitaries, military officers, local officials, tri-D cameras and crews, brass bands, flag dancers, and enough of the general public to provide an endless sea of faces and a steady cacophony of voices under the stirring martial music, the officers and men of the U.S.S. *Skipjack* were to be decorated.

The captain of *Skipjack*, Paul Riker, stood erect under Xhole's hot blue sun, flawlessly turned out in dress whites, his tightly bandaged arm in a close sling. His forehead was wet under the leather band of his hat, and little beads of dampness dotted his upper lip, stinging where he had shaved too close. His face felt flushed and moist. He sneaked a glance at Dao Marik, his Einai Science Officer, who was standing at his right hand, and envied the cool composure of the man who, among all of them, had lost the most in this operation. With that knowledge came a familiar wash of guilt, and he squinted against the hot blue glare and tried to ignore the tri-D camera that was getting a tight head shot of him for its viewers. The music was too loud, too strident. There was the smell of warm brass polish, hot oil, and rocket exhaust in the air. Heat rose in barely visible waves from the quarter-deck. Marik, green-gold in his immaculate white uniform, seemed wavering and unreal. Flag dancers, whirling their red and yellow banners. Really very warm out here. Timbrels. Lyres. The captain wondered what, if anything, Marik would be think-ing just about now. Hot, really.

Marik, alert to his captain's condition, saw him sway slightly where he stood and steadied him with an unob-trusive hand at his elbow. The camera moved in to high-light this assistance, and Marik resented it, thinking iron-ically how pathetic they both must look, he with his cane and his limp, and Paul with his dignified sling. Paul had no business out here. What he needed, what they all need-ed, was rest. Someplace quiet where they could go—and lie down—and sleep—for a hundred years, if need be! Trumpets blared past, gleaming. How brave it all was, Marik thought, and for himself, at least, how utterly useless. Although, he reflected, they had saved the race called the Ungt—and most of the crew. They had lost very few men.

And only one woman.

One small woman.

He did not think of the woman.

The speeches were interminable, and after those there were musical selections by the fleet concert band, while Marik's legs became a silent shriek, and the white-clad crew stood at attention and sweated, and the crowd milled and clamored, and somewhere hot-dog and popcorn ven-dors plied their ancient trade and stale wares among the multitude.

Earlier, in cool, stained-glass, beeswax silence, three bishops had concelebrated the Solemn Mass of the Un-born; but afterward, it was a Shimshen choir (Mishli had been a Shimshen, dedicated to Life) that chanted the age-old litany that antedated the return of the Erthlikli and, indeed, the discovery of Eisernon itself.

There were sixteen Shimshenli, wearing the long iridescent habit bound at the waist with the narrow chain each Shimshen forged for herself. The lower half of their faces was painted the familiar pale-blue caste mark of their order, and their voices, chanting first mother, now child, were alien and angelic.

Cantor:	From ignorance and fear,
	Oh, Lord, deliver us!
Response:	*Oh, Lord, deliver us*
	From death before birth!
Cantor:	From the barrenness of vanity,
	Oh, Lord, deliver us!
Response:	*Oh, Lord, deliver us*
	From the slaughter of the unborn!
Cantor:	From the will of the child killers,
	Oh, Lord, deliver us!
Response:	*Oh, Lord, deliver us*
	From the scalpel of the excutioners!
Cantor:	From the hatred of our forebears,
	Oh, Lord, deliver us!
Response:	*Oh, Lord, deliver us*
	From those who labor to bring
	forth death!
Cantor:	From the Mark of Medea,
	Oh, Lord, deliver us!
Response:	*Oh, Lord, deliver us*
	From the Hand of Herod!

"That the cries of the innocent come unto thee," chanted the cantor in the voice of every mother.

"We beseech thee, hear us," came the many-voiced response.

"That the promise of the unborn be fulfilled," the cantor persisted evenly.

"We beseech thee, hear us," returned the steady cadence.

Riker leaned toward Marik, hairs prickling the back of his neck.

"Are they speaking for the *fetuses?*" he asked in an incredulous whisper, and Marik nodded once, impressively, and whispered, "They cannot speak for themselves, sir."

"We beseech thee," chanted the children's voices. "Hear us."

Neither could Hennem-mishli speak for herself, the captain realized with a start. Not when she had the Ungt children to speak for, to preserve; and he understood an edge, an inkling, of why she had elected to stay behind, in lieu of those children. For an instant he felt a kind of joy, almost a jubilation, that he and Marik had permitted her to stay; and then he saw again in his mind's eye Marik's scorched, desperate face when he, Riker, had forbidden him at gunpoint to stay in her stead and felt again the crushing wave of guilt that had plagued him since the rescue.

Marik would have let him shoot him; he knew that now. To the Einai's rational, alien mind, it would have solved the whole problem. But Riker, clever Riker, had held the gun on Mishli, thereby killing something, he was not quite sure what, in himself—or in Marik—or in what he had been pleased to regard as their friendship.

And, of course, Mishli.

"Marik," he ventured huskily, staring straight ahead at the approaching dignitaries, "forgive me—will you?"

At that, the Einai glanced at him quickly, perplexed.

"For what, sir?"

He doesn't know, Riker marveled. He actually doesn't know. Marik's alienness was never more evident than in the fact that he truly did not know why Riker would need his forgiveness; or that there was anything to forgive. An earthling would know, Riker mused; he would know and stew about it and hate and fester and one day maybe blow the ship and himself to kingdom come. Either that, or he would sign on another vessel and spend the rest of his days pickling his worthless carcass in cheap booze, talking down *Skipjack* in general and Paul Riker in particular.

But not Marik. Marik considered the incident closed. He had come to sickbay and made it clear that Riker had done his duty to the ship and the crew, sir; and Mishli had remained true to her vow, which superseded their relationship by nature and by God, and that he quite understood. Riker was not to fret about it. Thank you, sir.

It was much later that Riker discovered, quite by accident, that had Marik not assisted with his surgery, he, Riker, would have lost the arm.

Marik was still watching him concernedly out of the tail of his eye, and Riker wanted to say something—anything!—to him; but then the admiral and his entourage were there, and Riker knew he could never bring up the subject again.

The lean, taut old man in the white uniform smiled and said the things required of him to say about bravery and dedication and leadership and how proud the service was, first of himself—the medal pinned on easily, he shook hands, saluted, braced up—and of Marik—same medal, same speech, same slick salute.

There was a moment's embarrassed hesitation when the Old Man presented Marik with the second medal, the posthumous medal for Hennem-mishli, Shimshen to the Ungt.

"I suppose this one should go to you, Mister Marik. She would have wanted you to have it."

No, she wouldn't, Marik thought. She would have clowned with the medal, laughing softly, and put it away somewhere. Marik gazed straight ahead, at the gold braid on the Old Man's hat brim.

"Yes, sir. Thank you, sir."

"I hope you'll accept my sympathies. She was your wife, wasn't she?" He had lowered his voice confidentially.

"Yes, sir." On the far edge of the crowd, the flag dancers were furling their flags, getting ready to go home.

"She gave her life in a noble cause, young man. She and the others spared countless lives to come." He shook his head ruefully. "Too bad you couldn't save her."

"I could have, sir," Marik said quietly. "I could have forced her to come. I did not."

The admiral shot a grim look at his aide, a beefy, jowled rear admiral whose jaw set hard; cleared his throat, made an effort to be calm, and glared directly into the alien's grey, slit-pupiled eyes.

"Do—you—mean—to—tell—me," he measured his words to the millimeter, "that *you*—left *your wife* there —to be vaporized by a *sun!*—when you could have spared her that!"

"Yes, sir." Composed. Remote.

The eager cameras leaned close to stare, to eavesdrop,

and in their homes, people leaned forward, too, not to miss a sound.

"Why?" The word exploded from the Old Man's lips like an epithet.

"She had made a vow, Commodore. It was her place to be."

The Old Man's voice shook with barely controlled rage, and a blue vein in his temple, under the close-cropped white hair, thudded rapidly.

"That, sir," he ground out, "is one of the most cold-blooded statements I have ever heard made by civilized man! In the name of God, man, what does a vow mean under circumstances like that! Hell's bells! Break it! You could've broken it!—to save her life! What kind of man are you!?" He leaned close, shaking with ill-controlled fury. "If you will forgive me, Mister Marik, it is just such attitudes that cause many of us to consider your species inferior!"

There were other presentations that day, but Marik did not hear them. Over the crowds and the loudspeakers and the metallic anthems, he only heard the low, soft strumming of her *chukuri* and the quiet music of her voice.

Chapter I

The summers on Eisernon are hot. Hot and humid, with sunlight as thick and heavy as beaten metal, aun hives murmuring in the fern forests, and dakan flowers fragrant on the gentle air.

Summer aboard the U.S.S. *Skipjack* was, for the Einai officer called Dao Marik, a notation on the fascia chronometer, an air-conditioned, utilitarian, sunless grind of work, eat, work, sleep, work, and standing extra watches to ensure himself of no time to think. One mustn't think. Bad idea, thinking. Could get you into a lot of trouble. Better to just go along, see to the ship, perform one's duties with that inhuman precision the Erthlikli expected of an alien officer, and keep one's mouth shut.

But don't think. Never think. It was the thinking that got to you.

Take the crew, for instance. The men had always treated him respectfully, if somewhat gingerly, and he had used his social exile to maintain an impartial justice in his dealings with them. (If this insular life provided him with more solitude than he cared to enjoy, he justified his loneliness by the knowledge that both the *Skipjack* and her crew were performing at optimum levels of efficiency and safety.)

Now all that was changed. The crew's courteous diffidence had become chill hostility, stopping just short of insolence; and while all he had encountered so far were scowls and sudden tense silences when he entered an occupied area, he had heard enough to realize that most of the men bitterly resented him and cursed him roundly among themselves. There was desultory talk in the wardrooms, too, and it filtered back. Any man, they said, who could sell out his wife (and such a pretty little wife, too) for a Federation Medal of Honor was just about as alien as they could stomach.

Some of them could not stomach that much. As Marik limped through the whispering portal onto the bridge, he caught the edge of the navigator's hateful thought even as the captain greeted him.

"Mister Marik, take a look at this. We've got a target, out here in the middle of nowhere, and we can't pick it up." He turned to the communications officer. "Anything, Jen?"

"No response, sir," she replied primly. "I sent 'routine patrol' and our identification, but—" She made a gesture equivalent to a shrug.

Space was a velvet black pit on the forward viewscreen, with sharp points of steady light marking out the stars. It shifted minutely as Marik, searching, adjusted the focus, adjusted once more—and stopped.

"I believe I have it, sir."

He sat slowly, intent upon his instruments, apparently unaware of the navigator's enmity, his surgeon's hands moving with cat's-paw delicacy across the board. Space shifted again, and yet again, very slightly, and a pale blur resolved itself into a small, blasted lifeboat of strange proportions and contour, floating dead in space.

"It's not one of ours, Paul," rumbled Simon MBenga.

"We still have no response, Captain Riker," Communications announced.

Riker, his gaze still fixed on the screen, merely tilted his head, and Marik's fingers flew over the console. Information chattered back.

"She's not registered with Lloyd's, sir."

"Check her with Jane's."

"Check coming in now. No, Captain. An unregistered vessel." He turned and regarded the screen through the clear, slit-pupiled grey eyes of the legendary Han Einai, and the navigator looked away uneasily and knocked on wood.

Paul Riker leaned back in his command chair and addressed his officers quietly. "Marik? Simon? What do you think?"

"Krail trap, maybe," guessed the huge black monolith who was the ship's Executive Officer. "Set us up, knock us out. They've tried it before."

"Possible. Marik?"

"Natural hazards, perhaps." His voice cooled. "Records show that this sector has been visited only once by a star class vessel. The Einai cruiser *Arnumatek* made an extensive survey less than one hundred solar years ago. Unfortunately, *Arnumatek* was lost, with all hands, before she could relay her information."

At the mention of *Arnumatek,* there was an uneasy stir among the bridge personnel, and the navigator, Parry Kaplan, whistled softly to himself and wheeled on Riker impulsively.

"Sir, isn't the *Arnumatek* the one whose captain steered her—" He broke off as Marik's head snapped up and fixed him with the full, unreadable impact of that catlike grey gaze. Riker gave them both a quick, expert scrutiny.

"Go on, Mister Kaplan," he prompted quietly. " 'Whose Captain steered her . . .' "

Kaplan ducked his head. "Into the sun, sir," he muttered uncomfortably. "Her captain deliberately steered her into the sun."

No one moved but Marik, who turned away abruptly and busied himself at his computer.

"Take us in closer, Mister Rutledge. Jen?"

She looked at him and shook her head, and Riker got up and crossed leisurely to Marik's station.

"Coming up on target, sir," Navigation reported.

"Standard approach, helm," he answered absently, and sat on the edge of Marik's console. The Einai continued his work in silence, ignoring his presence.

"Standard approach it is, sir."

Riker folded his arms and narrowed his eyes thoughtfully.

"Let's see," he mused aloud. "Arnumatek . . . that translates out to . . . 'has-no-fear.' Am I right?"

Marik coded a few indices and recorded them permanently. "Your word 'valiant' would be more accurate, Captain," he answered in a preoccupied murmur.

"And she surveyed *this* sector."

"Yes, sir." Patiently. He resumed his coding.

"And she was lost," Riker persisted. "Why?"

Marik shut his eyes briefly. "Mister Kaplan seems to believe that her captain deliberately destroyed her, sir. That *is* the common impression."

"But the truth, Marik. What's the truth?"

It was clear that the captain did not intend to be put off, and Marik sighed, switched his panel to automatic, and faced him reluctantly. His tone was so confidential as to be almost inaudible.

"You will recall, sir, that my honored father was a member of the Einai senate"—Riker nodded once—"and as such, he had access to certain files and information that were not necessarily in the public domain. So it follows—" He paused to regroup. "Perhaps you will understand that in a Han family, which is a telepathic, as well as a social and genetic unit, while we have a term for 'privileged information,' there is no concept for 'secret.' There couldn't be. It has nothing to do with Security," he added rather defensively.

"I quite understand, Mister Marik. No problem."

Marik hesitated, this self-revelation obviously painful to him, especially with half the bridge frankly eavesdropping; then he continued with a good deal of restrained intensity. "Some information did get back. A message torp, badly battered. The captain of the *Arnumatek* was not trying to destroy his ship when he headed into Antilia. He was avoiding—" He broke off, flushing. "He was taking evasive action."

Riker threw a quick, reflex glance at the viewscreen and its innocuous-looking target. "Against what danger?"

Marik's pupils dilated with the intensity of his emotion.

"The dragons, Captain," he said softly. "Here there are dragons."

There was a general exhalation of held breaths, and someone chuckled derisively under his breath, but Riker,

18

knowing Marik, kept silent, while the individual hairs prickled the back of his neck.

"Superstition," he speculated. "Maybe the torp's message was garbled."

"The word 'dragon' was unmistakable. On five separate occasions." His slight accent gave it a singular chill. *"Dragon."*

Riker rose to his feet and retorted crisply, "And you didn't feel such information was important enough to include in your report, mister?"

Marik's eyes held him fast. "Would you have believed me if I had, sir?" he challenged soberly.

"Coming up on target," noted the helm.

Riker shook his head. "Probably not. I'm not sure I believe you now. But I should have been told." He strode across the bridge and flung himself into the command chair.

"All stop. Make ready the starboard tractors. Guns, arm the laser banks and stand by." He hit the com stud. "This is the captain. All hands go to yellow alert. Go to yellow alert.

"Mister Kaplan," he continued briskly, "get a wide-range scan going. Full sweep. If we're being set up for a Krail ambush, we'll want plenty of warning."

"Vessel hard abeam, sir," MBenga announced. "Laser banks armed and ready."

"Stand by. Marik, get a boarding party suited up. Find out what's going on over there. Among other things, I want to know why we can't scan that boat."

"Aye, sir." He limped noiselessly across the room and was gone.

As the portal hissed shut behind him, Simon MBenga gave a short, uneasy laugh and said, "I trust those *dragons* won't get him."

To which Kaplan, who had watched his exit with hot, angry eyes, replied, "I hope they do. Whatever they are— I hope they get him good!"

"That will be all, gentlemen," the captain said.

Space was clean and open and uncaring, and Marik stepped off the edge of the airlock into an endless well of stars. Stars like a silver rain, in every direction, and galaxies spiraled argent beyond them.

Mishli.

Behind him, silent in their white, face-plated suits, two well-armed security men pushed off the edge and followed him. The three of them were alone out here, totally alone, three bits of organic flotsam, connected only by the continuous white sound inside their headphones. It was a different silence than the one aboard, not hostile or guarded; merely vast and impersonal. The impersonality helped. It was good to be out here. Restful. Even the strange lifeboat, blotting out constellations dead ahead, seemed remote and of little import. Marik absently assisted his velocity with a short, bilateral burst of his belt chargers.

Nice out here. Quiet. Lonely. Although, he reflected, any place in the universe was lonely without Mishli. Every place.

Mishli, whom he had loved.

Mishli, who had lost her life, her precious life, consumed by a nova.

He gazed pensively around at the jewel-box stars, strewn with omniscient abandon across the universe, and wondered which constellation, which star, burning brightly, was hers.

"Watch it, Mister Marik!"

The security guard's warning came a moment too late, and Marik was aware of the lifeboat's hull plummeting toward him only seconds before it hit. He threw himself into a gymnast's tumble and met the boat feet first with a tremendous, bone-jarring impact, the pain buckling his knees and smashing them into the metal. His hands smarted and throbbed inside the heavy gloves, and for a moment his vision greened over sickly. He was dimly aware of the boat receding as he bounced languidly away, and he reached out, grabbed a projecting limb of metal, and clung to it with all his strength until his head cleared and the agony in his legs became bearable.

The two security men had hit the boat, too, though less violently, and there were dull thumps and muffled imprecations in his ears. As they subsided, Marik steadied himself and asked, as evenly as he could manage, "Any damage?"

"No, sir," snapped back the first cold reply, and the second man, a fellow named Kopicek, ventured, "You okay, Mister Marik?"

Marik, shaking uncontrollably from the shock of the

massive hull against his once-shattered legs, replied in the same, level tone, "Yes. Carry on."

He tried to pass a hand across his face to wipe away the chill sweat but encountered the face plate, and he smiled wryly to himself. Instead, he moved it, shakily, across the metal hull he lay against, the mirror reflecting himself and the stars as if he were trying to erase one or the other.

"Looking for a hatch, Mister Marik?" Kopicek offered, and Marik nodded shortly.

"Yes. A hatch. You men check her port side and underbelly."

"Did you see this baby move?" Kopicek demanded excitedly of his companion through the headset, even as they started around the prow. "She must'a shot up thirty meters! Just spunked up and jumped! Hit him like a ton of bricks! You should'a seen it!"

"I saw it," his companion answered irritably. "I saw it awready!" His attitude became formal. "Nothing so far, sir."

Marik, feeling along the seamless hull for a crevice that would indicate an entry, paused. *Odd sensation, as of a half-heard sound, or the first tentative brush of telepathic contact.* He dismissed it as nothing.

"I betcha somebody's in there," Kopicek mumbled. "One of them Krail, that's what I think. Hey, Mister Marik, how 'bout we just broach this hull and evacuate the cabin? That'll calm 'em down, hey, Peccora?"

A docking stanchion, oddly made, that lifted out of an invisible groove in the curved surface, the slick, featureless skin marred only by blackened stains, a line—

"Yeh, yeh, Kopicek, *domani*, eh?"

A *line*.

A line, a line, line, line, line. Follow it down, down, there it is, curved, yes, curved, curving—

"I've got it."

He heard the others' hurried approach even as his eager hands followed the line in its infinitesimal arc, its delicate depression. His hand slipped in where there was no "in," where there was no place for anything to go in or under or through, yet here was the edge of his hand, gone "into" the hull. He pushed it into the narrow aperture, feeling for a lock, a switch that must be there. There

21

—something—too far to reach, just beyond the tips of his fingers.

"Give me a tool. Anything. Something narrow."

They fumbled with gloved hands among the harnessed tools and came up with a wrench. Marik shook his head.

"No go. It won't reach. Give me that long Phillips."

The asterisk-ended shaft screeched against the metal (or would have, had there been air to carry the sound), and little flakes of the silvery metal fell on Marik's hands; but the tip reached the lock and tripped it, and the hatch flew open suddenly and swung slowly, almost leisurely, out into space, caught by its hidden hinges, the screwdriver floating lazily after it.

The interior of the airlock was dark and small, with a slender, windowless inner hatch that was fitted with a virtually invisible seam. They entered cautiously, Marik leading, the others following with drawn sidearms.

"Good workmanship, anyhow," Peccora commented. "Nothing shoddy about these guys."

There was a panel beside the door—Marik was unaccountably reminded of an Erthlik *mezuzah*—and when they stepped on a pressure plate, it lit up, revealing a few terse hieroglyphs. No one recognized the language. Marik tilted his head like a cat, listening.

"Eisernai, sir?" Kopicek asked.

"Not ours," Marik said absently. "Swing that hatch to."

"*Close* it, sir? The outer hatch?"

Marik motioned it shut, still watching that inner hatch, and Kopicek reluctantly pulled it shut, cutting off the faint starlight. There was a tiny sibilance of gas entering the chamber, and Peccora's torch leaped into startled light, making a flat, luminous disc on the deck. It leaped about, finding nothing. It was very quiet. The suits were hot and close. Nothing moved. Even Marik was dead still, like something watching a mouse hole. The hissing stopped.

Marik calmly leaned his weight against the hatch, and it gave easily, opening onto a Stygian, tangible blackness in which something rustled, and was still.

Two new lances of light, Marik's and Kopicek's, stabbed into the darkness and pooled there, revealing only bare deck with peculiar oval depressions set into it at regular intervals. The indentations were large, almost big enough to accommodate a small man, and lined with—

22

Marik knelt—a soft, fibrous substance he did not recognize. The overhead was so low they had to move in a permanent semicrouch, and the few bits of instrumentation, located between and inside the forward pair of depressions, was meaningless. Two or three curious mechanical devices and several bags of what appeared to be dry leaves or vegetable waste completed the contents of the boat. The hull was intact and the fittings sound.

Marik's headphones beeped.

"Marik."

"Riker here. What've you got?"

The not-sound again. The mental scent of *presence*. And of desperation. Whoever he was, the occupant of the lifeboat was still here. And he was in trouble.

"Stand by one, Captain." To Peccora, "Check around again. Someone is here. In the boat."

The headphones picked up his breathy exasperation, but Peccora obediently explored the cabin once again, stamped around in the depressions, flashed his torch up the walls and into the empty airlock behind them. But there was nothing. No one.

He bounced slowly back to Marik, spreading his hands expressively.

"Nothing, Mister Marik. Unless you wanta take some garbage aboard." He nudged one of the plastex sacks lightly with his boot, and the boat leaped and bucked, throwing them convulsively against deck and bulkhead. An explosive grunt, and Kopicek's torch lens smashed silently into little glittering pieces that kaleidoscoped apart, and Marik's medikit skittered noiselessly away across the wall. He dived after it even as his headphones crackled.

"Marik, what's going on over there? Report, mister!"

He caught the kit and brought up heavily against the curved, featureless nose plates, facing about slowly.

"Marik!" his headphones insisted. "Did you find anyone?"

Behind him, the plastex bags floated lazily into the center of the cabin and drifted aimlessly about. One of them was moving, ever so slightly, by itself.

"Yes, sir," Marik grinned triumphantly to himself. "Yes, sir, I believe we have."

"What it is," Neal Anderson explained to Riker, gesturing for emphasis with his cold pipe, "is an alien. I don't mean a regular, ordinary humanoid alien, like Marik or Miss Jen—I mean a real alien. An *alien* alien. This thing breathes methane, and it doesn't have any feeding apparatus, and what looks like overlapping dry leaves is really, well, sort of vibratory mechanisms."

Ben Morrison, standing there with his hands thrust into the pockets of his lab coat, muttered, "Marik is alien enough for me," and his chief gave him a dirty smile around the stem of his pipe.

"Well, Ben, then I'll feel safe leaving the experimental animals in your capable hands while Mister Marik and I take care of our visitor." Morrison started to protest, but Anderson put up a restraining hand.

"No, no. Don't thank me. Just—take good care of the rats and monkeys. I'll let you know how we make out."

Morrison's reply, as he left, was unintelligible.

"He's a good man," Anderson continued mildly to Riker, "but he's a helluva bigot. Come on, I'll show you what we're doing in here."

Riker stopped him. "Neal. This Marik thing. It's really got me concerned."

Anderson took the pipe out of his mouth and considered his answer for a long moment while pretending to examine the pipe stem.

"You're going to have to let it blow over. Ride it out. You can't blame the men. They all knew her; half of them fancied they were in love with her." He shrugged, as if to say, What more can you expect? Riker struck the bulkhead with the edge of his hand.

"He's tearing up the ship!"

Neal dropped his eyes, saying nothing, and Riker shook his head.

"No. That's not true." He shook his head again quickly, squinting at the deck. *"I'm* tearing up my ship, Neal! Because I let Marik take the responsibility for my decision!" He looked at Anderson with a kind of bewildered horror in his eyes. "Good God, what have I done?"

"You've made a command decision, Captain," Anderson retorted bluntly, feeling that a dash of cold water was in order just about now, "and I suggest you stick with it. Now, would you like a report on that alien or not? You're wasting my valuable time." His big bulk was oddly reassuring, there in the narrow corridor. Riker smiled briefly, without humor.

"Right with you." He made a gesture of "after you" and followed Anderson through the ward and into the makeshift ICU.

Stick with it, Anderson had said. You made a decision, now stick with it. You can hold your friend at gun point and forbid him to give his life in exchange for his wife's life because it was good for the ship, because they needed Marik's cool, alien reasonableness and his medical skill and his scientific knowhow. Now the ship was breaking up because of it, because the men did not know how it had been, or why the serene, grey-eyed little alien lady would give up her life for a carton of fertilized eggs. Fetuses. Children.

Marik understood, and in his own way, Riker thought, he forgave him. But he was the only one who did. Least of all, himself.

Stick with it, Anderson had said, and Riker chuckled bitterly. He had no choice.

Now, and probably forever, he was stuck with it.

The alien thing was injured. Marik, leaning both hands on the bunk beside it, could feel its blurred, incoherent misery even though the two could make no verbal contact. Here it lay, isolated from its own kind and the Erthlikli alike, a cylinder of methane gas slowly feeding into the plastex wrapping that was its spacesuit. They dared not tamper with that, even though it was torn and leaked in half a dozen places. They had carefully analyzed and supplemented its air supply, made it as comfortable as possible, and immobilized it. There was not much else they could do until the lab work came back. It would not be long in coming.

Marik did the preliminary physical and workup himself, not trusting it to the eager, curious medics because he was logically the most eminently qualified to handle it. His being both the ship's science officer and a Priyam (which calling transcended that of the Erthlik physician at roughly the same ratio as the physician's superseded that of a witch doctor) made it unthinkable for anyone else even to try it. That Marik would be attending physician was a foregone conclusion, and they hated him for it, but it was the only thing they could have done. None of the others would even have known where to start.

Marik knew, and it was a task of no little fascination. While he dared not use X ray or lascan, there being no data available on the being's radiation tolerance or light sensitivity, a careful check, painstakingly measured with calipers and dutifully recorded on tape, revealed the absence of a bony cranium and vertebral column—

discount possibility of counterpart mammalia aves pisces and related branches stop rule out insecta arthropoda and related branches stop

—with a correspondingly tough fibrous membrane apparently covering the brain proper—

large, well-developed frontal lobes somewhat shrunken stop rule out neoplasm stop rule out viral and/or bacterial infection stop rule out radiation damage stop

—under slick, movable skull plates of the same inert substance as those that covered the body like overlapping dry leaves. These were large, stiff, spatulate scales of veined translucent blue mail that might be a means of speech or camouflage or protection against natural enemies; there was no way to tell. It was probably none of them.

Marik photographed them, clipped a small sample and did a frozen section, but it revealed only that there had once been a venous circulation of sorts throughout the scale, and that it had now ceased, which, he surmised, accounted for its brittleness.

The head boasted two pairs of large, many-faceted eyes, which dominated a band across the front and both sides, but no tympanic membranes or external nares. As Marik tested the eyes and meticulously recorded his findings, a wicked little part of him was reminded of the med student who, performing his first alien cadaver dissection and having found no external nares, concluded that the being could not smell; whereupon, an Erthlik upperclassman, wise to the lore of the antiquated dissection lab, invited him to stick around until midsummer and test his theory.

He eased his head back, resting his tense neck; when the mind started sneaking stale old medical school jokes in on you, it was time to work a few kinks out. He stretched luxuriously as far as the isolation suit would permit, lazily, like a big cat, and bent to his task again, curiously refreshed.

A few delicate antennae sprouted like individual plumes from the convex area where a mouth should have been, and below them was an intricate, frilled aperture fitted internally with—Marik probed gently, peering close, and the creature flinched, as if in pain—six bands of elastic tissue resembling cartilage that crossed the lumen of the organ in parallel pairs. A marked puffiness and discoloration, possibly indicative of bruising, distorted the left lateral pair.

Interesting. This would bear closer examination when they got around to doing a post-mortem on the bodies still in the lifeboat; if, indeed, they got the opportunity. The sub's facilities for that sort of thing were markedly limited.

A warm breath exhaled constantly through the opening, making a faint, low-pitched hum, although the creature's primary breathing apparatus was clearly defined by a twin row of operative spiracles ranged along either side of the abdomen. A check of the "lungs" sounded heavy and wet; possibly a normal state of affairs, but Marik did not think so. Air moving in and out of any healthy breathing cavity had business to be relatively moist and quiet—there should not have been that tight, wet wheezing. He wondered uneasily how one would go about treating pneumonia in a creature that was as total a stranger as anyone—or anything—was likely to get.

He reached for a stack of agar plates, held one over each of the being's spiracles until it had been properly breathed upon, covered it, and marked it for incubation. He repeated the process with beef-blood medium and a neriosh gel, then took a sample of the gelatinous exudite from the edge of a partially obscured spiracle and incubated that, too, while he programmed the Medicomp from the lab terminal. That done, he relaxed his thoughts and tried, fairly successfully, to establish an emotional contact with the being. It clung weakly to his mind like an unconscious humanoid patient grasping any hand that was offered him. But there was little chance, Marik felt, for any real mental link. It was far too alien for that.

Strange creature. It was buglike, yet there were those large frontal lobes which argued for intelligence. It was warm-blooded, after a fashion, for it maintained its own moderate temperature without resorting to ambient heat; but there was no circulatory system as we know it. It breathed, but it neither ate nor excreted.

It was a fascinating enigma, and Marik fervently wished for the time and equipment to autopsy one of the bodies from the lifeboat. He had a nagging suspicion growing at the back of his mind that wondered where—in this galaxy, at least—creatures such as this could have evolved; or whether they might not be more alien than anyone had guessed.

"Anything new?" Neal Anderson, suited and masked like Marik, entered the ICU and crossed to the bunk. Beyond him, through the transparency, Marik could see a small crowd of medics and crewmen, among them Paul Riker, who stood watching them with a concerned expression.

"Everything," Marik answered, studying the CRT display. The curt terms were written in light letters on the black screen:

```
!MEDICOMP
@MAKE STRANGER
.ASSIGN "SCAN" TO ISOLATION—ICU
.FULL PRINTOUT ON PRINTER
.FULL ANALYSIS
.ANALYZE
.PRINT
.END
.
@EXECUTE STRANGER
. . . SCAN ASSIGNED
? ? TOO MUCH CORE USED—JOB ABORTED
@
```

Marik sighed. "Medicomp's no help. The program's too complex. It's taking too much core space." He hit the wall stud and saw the red light blink at the corridor communicator.

"Paul, I've got to have more core. Can you go to a manual helm?"

Riker shook his head at him through the transparency. "Negative. We've delayed warp, and we're still having to compensate from the bridge. I can't afford any more three-second command delays. You've diverted all the K possible and then some."

"What about Environmental Control?"

Riker narrowed his eyes. "It's that important."

"At least."

"How long would it take? Conservatively."

Marik hesitated, thinking fast. "Call it an hour."

Riker let the weight of his gaze (and with it, the weight of his command) rest evenly on Marik for a long moment. Then he nodded shortly.

"You've got it."

He repunched the communicator. "Computer."

There was a metallic chattering. *"Ready,"* said the inhuman voice. The ship waited.

"Release core storage for Environmental Control."

"Authorization."

"Riker, Paul. Captain, U.S.S. *Skipjack*."

The quick chitter of voiceprint match. A pause. *"Allocation released."*

Riker punched for sickbay and saw Marik hit the stud. "Go," he said.

Marik typed the "execute" command for the "stranger" program, and before he lifted his hands from the terminal, the air-conditioning system faltered and shut down, and the corridor lights browned out to dull yellowish bands in the overhead. There was a perceptible lessening of the ship's artificial gravity, and Marik sensed a tinge of anxiety in his patient; he thought compassion at it, and quiet, and it subsided. The ship was oddly quiet, as if the silence of the still air was somehow louder than the air in motion and demanded the attention.

The computer, at last drawing full measure of power and core required for its intriguing problem, hummed about its work, correlating and cataloguing, fitting old concepts into new and unfamiliar parameters and setting new parameters.

While it worked, Marik busied himself in taking another small sample of the being's overlapping scales. He tagged part of it for later testing and immersed the remainder in a concentrated hydrochloric acid solution, hoping to separate the chitin, if that is what it was, from the proteins and inorganic salts that would be linked to it. He could analyze proteins, identify salts, and in that way perhaps

29

come to some conclusion regarding his patient's malady, and, more importantly, its treatment. In the few hours he had been treating it, it had grown slowly, steadily weaker. The purring exhalation of gases through its frilled cranial vent had become inaudible, and even its strange mental patterns carried a peculiar "double vision" effect, as if he were sensing two identities instead of one. Schizophrenia? he wondered, and quickly relegated the possibilities to his own mental hinterlands. He had enough trouble trying to heal it physically without venturing into the chaos of alien psychiatry.

He checked the incubator. While neither the agar plates nor the neriosh showed any evidence of growth beyond a tentative hint of a pale fur, the beef-blood medium was growing merrily. On a hunch, he pulled down a Petri dish containing NNN medium, inoculated it with a sample of the being's gelatinous exudite, and shoved that into the incubator, too. He recorded time, medium, procedure in the medical log, eager to get to work on the bacteriology of the creature; but in the end he elected to wait for optimum isolation conditions before he tried to stain out any slides for examination. Isolation aboard the *Skipjack* was makeshift, at best; let some sort of exotic microorganism loose aboardship, with no possibility of anyone's being immune, and you could precipitate all sorts of nasty, virulent mutations and take out quite a few men. He wondered idly if he would be among them, and on the strength of that conjecture, prepared a culture of his own blood and inoculated that, too. It would be interesting to find out.

Anderson was hunched over the viewscreen when he stepped back into sickbay proper, watching the boarding party strip the alien lifeboat of everything portable. Crewmen, like so many white ants, crawled across its flanks and scrambled through its open hatches, only to re-emerge moments later bearing away portions of its viscera. Last of all to be brought away were the three plastex-suited corpses of the alien's shipmates. These they stowed in the cargo hold, where no temperature-control servos mitigated the utter cold. Marik had asked that they be salvaged for autopsy, and so, swearing roundly and jerking the bodies along, the men hauled them aboard. Some of the comments made were so specifically derogatory of Marik that

30

Anderson coughed loudly to cover them and switched off the screen.

"Well," he asked, a shade too heartily, "you just about finished in there?"

The grey cat eyes lingered on the darkened screen for a moment longer, then glanced at the incubator. Marik almost smiled.

"Not quite," he answered softly. "I'm not quite finished —in there."

Anderson, flustered, glanced at his ticket. More than a timepiece, the ticket was virtually an artificial appendage. Without one, you not only didn't get to practice whatever medical or paramedical profession you had been trained for, you didn't get beyond the loading platform at the shuttle bus. The only personnel who got aboard a hospital ship—or into sickbay—without a ticket came in through the cargo hold, feet first. Inpatients were issued tickets before their wounds were bound up; outpatients were given disposable tickets of two-hour duration. They took no chances. The Federation had learned its lesson in the Great Epidemic of Ferret I. It would never happen again. It could never be allowed to happen again. The tickets were one means of preventing it.

Anderson's ticket read biologically clean and normal and showed an elapsed time for the computer program as 00:54:07.

"We're about ready for that printout, aren't we?" he ventured, and as if in reply to his query, the terminal slot hummed importantly and put out a long white tongue of paper, which Anderson tore off and held up to the light. He looked at Marik sharply, admiringly.

"Damn! You're thorough enough! Listen to this: Uh, wait a minute, now, methane, swamp gas, uh, huh, wait a minute, okay, here—'being evinces certain characteristics of various *Arthropoda* and/or *Insecta*, especially in the area of vibratory apparatus, which may parallel flight apparatus of *Apis Mellifera*, which see.' That's a bee," he added unnecessarily to Marik, over the top of the paper.

"And it goes on, here— This is the interesting part. 'Recommend investigation of subject's home world as probably extragalactic planet. See Charts SC 1683 and SC 1689, respectively—' and so forth," Anderson finished. "An extragalactic alien! What do you think of that?"

31

"Remarkable, sir. You'll contact *Hope*, of course?" Coolly.

"Hm?" Anderson, rereading the tape, wagged his head delightedly and, grinning around the stem of his pipe, looked up blankly.

"The *Hope?* Well, of course, the *Hope*, Marik; f'God's sake, this is the find of the century! This changes history! Paul!" He hurried into the decon chamber, stood under the flash, stomped out of his isolation suit, and burst into the corridor waving the tape at the captain. Riker scanned it, and after a brief, animated discussion, as seen through the transparency, he stared at Anderson, indicated Marik and the alien with one quizzical motion, and hit the switch of the communicator on the bulkhead.

Now, Marik mused, if we could only find out what this being is, and what it was doing out there, alone in space.

Us being the Elluvon, came the desperate, almost incoherent thought, *also us very important having gift for you.*

Marik quickly leaned over the cot and felt for some further telepathic contact, but there was, as usual, only the strange nonpattern of the alien's mental processes and a lingering echo in his own mind. It was as though a warm hand had touched him firmly on the arm, and even when it was no longer there, the sense of warmth and pressure remained.

The Elluvon, he thought. They call themselves the Elluvon.

Anderson reappeared, looking smug. He was freshly suited up, and he still had the stem—not the rest of it, just the chewed black stem—of his pipe between his teeth, there behind the face plate, and he rolled it to one side of his mouth and grinned at Marik.

"We got hold of the *Hope*. We're going to rendezvous in a little over an hour. We'll transfer you, me, and this being over there and see what we can do for it. Mike Sharobi's got the best facilities in the galaxy for this sort of thing." He poked uncomfortably at the alien for a bit. "I only wish I knew what the hell it is."

"It's an Elluvon," Marik told him. "And it says it has a gift for us."

Anderson froze and gazed fixedly at him, saying nothing.

"Although," Marik admitted soberly, enjoying himself

32

immensely, "it refers to itself in the plural, so perhaps I should say, 'they are the Elluvon, and they have a gift for us.' "

Anderson's expression, that of a mule hit between the eyes by a plank, did not change. He opened his stiff lips in a hoarse croak.

"I don't suppose you would know," he said slowly, "just what this 'gift' would be."

"No, Doctor."

"But you say it talked to you. It talked. To you."

"In a manner of speaking."

"That's not funny, Marik."

"It wasn't intended to be, Doctor. I was merely trying to convey data to you." But a certain feline humor lay behind the level grey eyes.

"Well, maybe you would like to explain just what manner of speaking you're referring to, since this thing doesn't have anything to talk with. Like a mouth or a discernible thorax or anything."

"It thought at me, Doctor," Marik said matter-of-factly, and at long last Anderson blinked. He closed his eyes. He opened them. Nothing else of him, for the moment, moved.

"Oh. Oh. Well. I see. I knew there had to be some kind of a reasonable explanation." He tried to take the pipe stem out of his mouth; discovered that it had fallen unnoticed and was rolling around the bottom of his helmet, inside the face plate; looked at the offending hand as if it were a puzzling new appendage; tried to rub the back of his tense neck and ended up stroking the nape of his isolation suit.

"One of these fine days," he said pleasantly to no one in particular, "I may go right out of my mind."

Marik had turned his attention to more important matters and did not hear him. For the alien—the Elluvon—who had been lying quietly until now, began to stir fretfully, and its abdomen, under the scaled armor, began to contract in that fluid, rippling motion one sometimes sees in caterpillars. The movement was slight but distinct and showed no sign of letting up. The Elluvon seemed to be in pain.

Marik lay a hand on the thick, coarsely "furred" tegument under the scales and, palpating carefully, discovered

33

a large, firm mass, approximately twenty by twenty-five centimeters, in a rough ovoid. It was impossible to estimate its thickness.

"Neal, have a look at this."

It was the first time Marik had used his given name, and to Anderson's surprise, it warmed him. He examined the mass deeply, a good deal less gently, and shot a glance at Marik, eyebrows climbing.

"I'd have to call it a tumor. No doubt about it."

"I'm not so sure." Marik closed his eyes and felt deeper, probing with his mind as well as with his hands, when suddenly, with startling clarity, he was on the power deck. For one long, luminous instant, he felt the great engines reverberating in his flesh, smelled the indefinable engine-room smells, heard Gerffert and Calkins arguing about the gravity loss and the sound of Jackson's *mau thargan* off somewhere. His attention was bent, forcibly bent, as if someone had pushed his face downward toward a spot on the deck beside the auxiliary helm. There was no difference in this particular bit of deck from any of the rest, but there was a wash of desperation—and not Marik's own desperation—when he failed to recognize the significance of the deck plate; and his mind was flooded—abruptly, violently flooded—with images, the impact and significance of which were so vivid and powerful they threatened to bowl him over physically.

Anderson's panicky voice seemed to come from a distant cave.

"Marik! Snap out of it, man! What's the matter?"

Marik tore himself free from the mental contact with a savage wretch and found himself standing rigidly at the edge of the cot, gripping the metal with white knuckles. His face was streaming with sweat, and his breathing was shallow and ragged. Anderson, obviously concerned, was shaking him hard.

"Come out of it! What's wrong? You sick?" He grabbed Marik's wrist and scrutinized his ticket. Nothing. Marik's hands were shaking.

"No. No, I'm"— he forced what he hoped was a reassuring smile—"I'm fine. I—I was concentrating. On the Elluvon, you know." He avoided Anderson's disbelieving eyes and spoke to the slender crystalline instrument he pulled from his belt clip.

34

"How long did you say it would take for rendezvous?"

The doctor continued watching him out of narrowed eyes. "About an hour, Paul says. Why?"

Marik calculated quickly and looked up. "On what course?"

Anderson shrugged. "Ask me the easy one, about brain surgery."

Marik frowned at the instrument, cleared it, and calculated again. The result was the same: Given the present speed and course, they could expect the rendezvous with the U.S.S. *Hope* to occur close upon dead center of the dragons' migration path. With what he had just seen—

"I've got to see the captain." He headed for the decon chamber, stripping off his gloves as he went. Anderson sauntered up as he stood under the flash, tugged his tunic over his head, drew on one boot.

"Marik?" The Einai officer paused, not looking up. It was obvious that he was still shaken. "Anything you want to tell me—about that in there?" He tipped his head toward the Elluvon.

Marik's head came up as if he might share a confidence. Indeed, he looked to be on the verge of relating the whole experience, whatever it might have been; then he shut his eyes, shook his head as if to clear it, and yanked on his other boot.

"I'm sorry, Doctor. Privileged information. Keep an eye on Elluvon for me, will you?"

He limped away like a crippled panther, and Anderson, with a distinct sense of having missed the whole point, paced the isolation unit back and forth a few times before coming to a stop beside the Elluvon. He watched it for a few moments with evident distaste, this being that had been his great triumph only an hour before, and grasping the edge of the cot, snapped crossly, "Well! Don't just lie there squirming, you great bag of garbage! *Do* something!"

And the Elluvon, cooperative to a fault, did.

Chapter II

The Elluvon armada was the most impossible and awe-inspiring sight any humanoid had ever seen. Marik, like most of the men of the Star Service, had witnessed fleet maneuvers many times and had been privileged, upon the occasion of the Federation's Bicentennial Anniversary, to view the entire assembled fleet, majestically cruising in tight formation at sublight speeds; and an impressive sight it was, a never-to-be-forgotten moment when the skies of every en route planet were filled from horizon to horizon with glistening white iotas and men's faces, unashamedly wet, turned up to watch them pass, and the pride of belonging to and sharing that vast glory made the heart swell until it felt it would burst.

But this: This was eerie and portentous, a sight to make the hackles rise and send an adrenalin chill along the hide, these ten thousand ships made of juggled blue balls of light, bristling with symbolic weaponry that had no basis in galactic technology and therefore precluded even the possibility of a counterweapon. There was no defense. The galaxy was helpless. Not only the powerful Federation, but the colonies, the StarBases, and even the wide-flung

Krail empire, stood empty-handed against the advent of the Elluvon.

"But what do they want?" Paul Riker, leaning forward across his desk, invaded Marik's eyes intently as if he could draw forth believable information by the sheer power of his will. Marik shook his head.

"I don't know, Paul. I honestly don't know. It all came so fast . . . You—you never actually expect anyone else to have such force, such—*power*." He pressed his interlocked fists against his forehead.

"I can tell you only this: Their armada is on its way! It is here! *I saw it!*" There was a pause, and he repressed a shudder and dragged himself back from the awesome memory. "What I saw may have been symbolic; it may have been purely from Elluvon's point of view, through its eyes alone, I don't know. But I know—*I know!*—that armada's coming. And I know those weapons work."

Riker tapped the desk with the edge of his hand and wet his lip in that odd, abstracted habit he had. "All right. All right, we have that much. Now what about this thing down in sickbay? Where does it fit in?"

"It—and its shipmates—were to have been our initial contact, I think. Elluvon, I believe, somehow more so than the others. It has to do with the 'gift.' And someone— maybe Krail, maybe . . . maybe anyone—got to them first."

Riker got up impatiently and strode around his quarters for a minute. He swung on Marik. "It's too thin. Com-Fleet'd never buy it. All we have to go on is the fact of that—that *thing* down there." He leaned forward. "Try to give me at least one hard fact: This Elluvon—is it an ambassador?"

"Liaison of some kind, I—I'm almost sure."

Riker struck the table. "You think! You believe! You're almost sure! I can't warp this ship on conjecture, mister! I'm trying to believe you, damn it. Give me something to go on!"

"There's nothing else I can tell you that would make any sense!"

"Then show me!"

Marik lowered his hands warily and gave a little involuntary shake of the head. There was in the room a sensation of drawing away, of muscles bunched and gathered.

Marik's voice, when he finally spoke, was low and husky. "You don't know what you're asking."

Riker had not moved, still that tough, eager stance. "Let's make that an order."

Marik dropped his hands and stood up in that fluid, balanced, inhuman motion of his, and his expression changed in a way that could not be expressed except to say that it deepened, that his guard fell, and for the first time, Riker saw the full, unrestrained alienness of the Han Einai, the unguarded totality of him, as other Han must see him. He nodded once, caught Riker's eyes and held them with such finesse, such easy force that Riker felt the first tinge of fear, but he fought it down and tried to stay calm as the first cool, inhuman tendrils of consciousness—*Marik's consciousness*—invaded his mind. *Impossible,* he thought, *unbearable*. It was not pain as we know pain, but such incredible *otherness* that it took all his strength to suppress a desire to fall back a step or two. He might have rescinded his order then, if he could have, but he found that he could not speak, or move, that his will had become very plastic and malleable, and the grey cat eyes dilated into black stars that pulled him swiftly, inexorably, down, stretched him interminably, limitlessly, like a long strand of viscous liquid, like honey poured cold from a stone jug into a bottomless black well, and he remembered from a hidden place in Marik's mind an old, old prayer, a half-remembered verse:

> I sing a Singularity in this and every other universe: That One and One and One make One, the multiplicity of Congruence that stretches such Conception from End to Endless End.

Paul Riker knew panic. He dropped through into blackness, and there was something terrible here, something unnatural and frightening and discordant with what the galaxy should be and look like. He could feel its dread with his stubborn Erthlik mind and with his keen, sensitive Einai mind, *but I'm Paul Riker, captain, U.S.S.* Skipjack, and *he's* the alien, and I— But he could not find the *I*, and that panicked him worst of all, and it was close and coming closer, and you could not understand it or fathom its reason, and he turned somehow and saw it, and panic became terror.

There, against the vast panoply of stars, in deepest space, danced the Elluvon armada.

It was unlike any armada he had ever seen, no orderly formations, no schooling of sleek white ships like untold minnows in a starry pond; this was insanity, idiocy piled on madness, an endless tumult of bobbing, tumbling, juggled balls of blue mist, transparent, featureless, disorderly, yet somehow sentient, and through Marik's mind he slipped into yet another mind—minds, thousands, billions of minds—all twisting, turning, spilling philosophy, greeting, caution, animosity, bending Riker's mind unmercifully into forms a human mind had never been intended to take. *I'm Paul Riker,* he shouted clinging to his sanity, *captain, U.S.S.* Skipjack. *I'm Paul Riker, captain, U.S.S.* Skipjack. But he was not. He was still Riker, back there somewhere, but he was Marik, too, and most terrifying of all, he was the armada. He not only saw and felt and knew it, he was *becoming* it, beginning to slip into the pattern—the non-pattern, or the very complex one—of slide, writhe, half-turn of a globe, and it started to become almost pleasant to let go, to merge, join, be absorbed and assimilated into this terrifying, delicious enigma . . .

The screaming saved him, snapped him back into himself, that and the pain in his head. Someone was screaming, full-throated, agonized screams, and there was a sudden mental release, a blessed aloneness in his mind, and he opened his eyes, gasping for breath, and discovered that he was still screaming. He silenced himself with an effort, fumbling clumsy hands over his open mouth, and felt his gorge rise.

"Oh, Jesus, Lord," he mumbled, "oh, Lord, God!"

He made it to the head just in time. After a while he rinsed his mouth and splashed cold water on his face with shaking hands. He did not see Marik, there behind the desk, until he fell over him. The Einai was crumpled on the deck, blood on his lip where he had bitten through it. He was so pale as to be frightening. It took some time to waken him, and when he finally opened his eyes, they were cold and empty, like a dark milk glass or the wax of a guttered candle; then he recognized Riker, and the mind behind the eyes began to burn through, warming them. He stirred. He touched his mouth and winced. "I'm sorry

39

—about that," he muttered thickly, "but—you asked for it!"

Riker laughed shakily, an edge of hysteria in it. "And I got it, too. Backfired, though, didn't it?" His hands would not stop shaking, and he clenched them together.

"You Erthlikli have the damndest minds!" Marik pulled himself into a chair, slid a slow glance his way, chuckled, and shook his head. "Do you know—that you actually—tried!—to join that—that *thing* out there?" He cradled his dark, close-cropped head in both hands and winced again. "How did you people—*ever!*—get out of the caves? Talpa men." It was the Einai equivalent of Neanderthalers, and Riker tried to answer, but his body was not working right; something was wrong, and the hideous image of those vaulting blue spheres kept sweeping him with unbeatable panic.

"M-Marik, I've got to tell you—" he began, but Marik cut him off with a morose, "I probably already know."

"You probably do," Riker expostulated, beginning to laugh unsteadily. "I won't have to talk at all anymore, just—" He made a gesture as of snatching something off the top of his head; and Marik, answering his whimpering laughter with a slow, sour grin, watched him keenly, analytically all the while. He welcomed Riker's poor attempt at humor. It was not funny, but in the light of their recent experience, it provided a welcome release, and they laughed companionably, Riker wiping his eyes repeatedly. It started as laughter; before Marik knew what was happening, it got out of hand. While his own reaction died down normally to an occasional chuckle, Riker's hilarity built and kept coming, stronger and wilder, like breakers, each surge more precarious, more damaging, than the last, with no end in sight. He shouted, roared, shook with laughter. He was convulsed with it, an explosive gale that had nothing to do with his numbed eyes and pale, strained face.

The realization that his captain was in shock fell upon Marik all at once, accustomed as he was to people of his own kind who could handle the strangeness of occupying another mind; he had lived with the ability since before birth, and the Elluvon had been a jolt even for him. It must have been sheer hell for Riker, for he had been not one mind away but two. The strain was about to break him. His laughter had gone beyond mirth, beyond hysteria: His face was the total and absolute caricature of a man shrieking for help. With a nice mixture of compassion and cold-blooded deliberation, Marik drew back his arm and struck his captain full in the face with all his strength. Riker laughed up at him insanely, and Marik hit him again, and again, until at last the laughter subsided into big, heaving sobs that racked his whole frame. While Riker pulled himself together, Marik pulled a decanter of brandy out of the bookcase, poured three fingers of it into a tumbler, and handed it to him. The glass rattled against his teeth and spilled down his chin, but he managed to get some of it down. Marik pulled a blanket off of the bunk and wrapped it around Riker's shoulders. The captain's hands were blue and shaking, his teeth were chattering, but his eyes were sane again. Marik touched his mind gingerly. Whole. Shocked, but sane. He breathed a little easier.

"Do you want a sedative, Captain?" Riker shook his head, never taking his eyes off him. He wiped his wet face with both hands and took a steadying deep breath.

"I-I'll be all right in a minute, I think. Marik?" The level gaze flicked to him and held. He swallowed past a dry throat. "Not a word about any of this until I give the okay, understand? We could panic the whole ship. The whole fleet!" His hands were beginning to steady. Marik flashed his brief, white grin. "Not likely, sir."

"What do you mean," Riker demanded testily, " 'not likely'?"

"They're Erthlikli, Captain. They'd simply choose not to believe me."

Riker opened his mouth to reply, but the communicator cut him off. A disgruntled Neal Anderson appeared on the screen. "Say, Paul— Well, f'God's sake, what happened to you? You look like old Billy Hell!"

"Did you want something, Neal?"

"Is Marik with you? I can't find him anyplace."

Marik stepped closer. "Right here, Doctor. What can I do for you?"

Anderson smiled mildly and winked both eyes in a gentle gesture that betrayed extreme annoyance to anyone who knew him. "You," he said, "personally!—can get your green-genius carcass down here, double-time, and tell me why a creature you swore could neither eat nor excrete—now, that's a direct quote, Marik!—has just delivered a seven-pound gelatinous mass smack dab in the middle of my nice, clean deck!"

Riker covered an unbeatable chuckle with a contrived cough and crossed to the other side of the room while Marik gazed mildly at the incensed doctor.

"The 'tumor,' I presume?" he inquired politely, and Anderson swore once, with great attention to detail and pronunciation, and rang off.

Marik turned to Riker and said, most sincerely, "I do hope it's benign."

Chapter III

The hospital ship called the U.S.S. *Hope* had once been a misfit, crewed and staffed by misfits. The sleek white ships of the fleet gave her wide berth when they intersected her course, and ComFleet barely acknowledged her existence; but she had been vital to the Federation, and they knew it. Embarrassing as it was—and it was—the rickety old bucket they called the good ship *Hope* was the only humane gesture the Galactic Federation had bothered to make in the two centuries of her existence.

Now all that had changed. For the past eight years, under the administration of Priyam Mykar Sharobi, the *Hope* had acquired the latest equipment, the finest staff, and a change of tenure, from the globular old tub the hospital had been occupying to the gleaming splendor of a mammoth starcruiser with multiwarp capabilities. Sharobi was under the impression, which he expressed publicly at every opportunity, that the preservation of life was paramount among mankind's most urgent requisites; and he was not shy about reminding senators and Federation delegates (many of whom knew him on a first-name basis) that should they ever require medical attention outside their own planetary jurisdiction, it would be the *Hope*, according, of course, to her facilities, that would try to keep them alive.

The enthusiasm of their collective response should not have been surprising, but it was. There was not anything Mike Sharobi could want for the *Hope* by way of equipment, supplies, or personnel that he did not get—and promptly! Moreover, that he had performed successful major surgery on two members of the Federation High Council was no detriment to his reputation; and while it was foreign to his nature to capitalize on his skill, it was widely rumored that the gift of the superb new operating facility aboard the *Hope* was being paid for by the good taxpayers of United Krau, and would be for some time to come.

Nor did Sharobi confine his interests to his own hospital: As Fleet Surgeon, chief of a mobile House, he made periodic rounds of the other hospitals and hospital ships, scrutinizing everything from their orderlies' fingernails to their surgeons' sutures. It was commonly said of Sharobi that if it were possible, he would pin every medical officer out on a tarpan and go through his guts with a probe; to which Sharobi, when he heard about it, was said to have remarked irritably that the notion of mere tarpans was sophomorically unimaginative. And outdated, too.

When word of the Elluvon hit the *Hope*, the two discrete segments of its population reacted characteristically: The crew mobilized its activities, much as a machine would silently and slickly shift into higher gear, charting course, rigging for warp, while scuttlebutt flew from bridge to quarter-deck to Black Gang, and everyone had his own theory of what the Elluvon had to be, or would look like, or what its purpose, if any, would turn out to be.

The medical staff, on the other hand, made preparations of its own. During regular running, empty wards were sealed off for economy of energy consumption. Because the *Hope* theoretically, at least, had facilities for every kind of known intelligent creature in the galaxy (and for some, Sharobi would have added sourly, that are pretty questionable), its energy demand was prodigious. Running with everything shut down but crew and staff quarters and the few occupied wards permitted *Hope* to go an entire solar year without refueling. By comparison, the *Skipjack*,

44

by reason of size and frugality, could go seven years, the length of a customary star run.

Now with the first extragalactic alien coming aboard, the hospital buzzed with activity. Isolation was set up for the methane breather and its gravity set at its probable norm of slightly less than earth-normal. The new operating facility was retooled for autopsy of the three Elluvon cadavers, and the extensive laboratories were ready for every study from gas chromatography to multiple lascan.

Senior nurses had switched shifts with less fortunate juniors, and Receiving was crowded with knots of staff men who pointedly discussed everything but the Elluvon. Interns, loitering as long as they dared in the corridors, discussed nothing else.

Medical engineers reprogrammed a MAX for the alien. Dietetics and Security were on standby.

The main Medicomp, which held the accumulated medical knowledge of the Galaxy and could be tapped from any ship or planetside terminal, had been brought up to full power, which was considerable. It was from the *Skipjack*'s input that the *Hope* drew Elluvon's requirements, and Sharobi, though it would have broken his teeth to say so, was pleased. He knew Marik, knew his work, and thought he had done a more than thorough workup, considering the outmoded equipment he had to work with. He considered asking again for Marik's transfer to the *Hope* and mentally filed it under "rethink." Brilliant as he was, if a request for transfer to *Hope* was not forthcoming from Marik himself, it would be worthless. The position Marik would fill was of sufficient status that it might be made available, but could never be offered. He wished Marik would ask. He wished they would hurry with the transporting—his palms itched to get into those cadavers and find out what the hell was going on. He wished he had beamed over himself so he could have hurried things along. It was not often that Mykar Sharobi found himself excited about anything, but the presence of an extragalactic alien in the house seemed a reasonable and uncommonly good excuse. He glanced around the empty corridor uneasily. He hoped no one had seen him pacing around. Regular jackass, he thought.

The idea of filterable virus occurred to him, and he rechecked the Isolation ward to make sure it had been

45

properly segregated by the biologically impervious seals built directly into the adjoining bulkheads. There were four such seals, each enclosing smaller segments of Isolation, with a full lab and galley set into each quarantined area. Should some lethal organism be accidentally transported aboard, it would be possible to effectively isolate whatever number of affected personnel necessary. The innermost lab, ward, and galley were completely automated in readiness for any really exotic organisms. No humanoid was required to risk his life in so grave a circumstance excepting the doctor on duty; and that, Sharobi growled to himself, was part of the job, anyway, and therefore inconsequential.

He patted the bulkhead. He was satisfied. The shields were safe.

The *Hope* came out of warp at the rendezvous point exactly one minute and forty-one seconds early, fully prepared for *Skipjack* and her unusual patient. Scanning, and finding nothing, she lay to and waited.

Skipjack arrived on time. Riker, who had a penchant for punctuality, sat regarding the screens with a mild surge of gratification as they dropped out of warp at precisely the appointed moment and got a fix on *Hope,* standing dead ahead.

"Captain." Simon MBenga's concern thrummed softly in the still air: Then he rechecked his instruments, frowning. "Thought I had a bogey, hard by, but it dropped out of sight."

"Stay on it. And post an extra watch on the scanners. I want to know everything that goes on out there." He thought again of the gyrating blue mists and clenched his teeth against the memory.

Parry Kaplan laughed shortly. "He'd better," he muttered to Rutledge. "Mister Marik's dragons might try to sneak up on us." The helmsman coolly replied that it wasn't ruddy likely, you know.

"But possible, Mister Rutledge," Riker said slowly, from a considerable mental distance. "Just—vaguely—possible." There was not much they could say about that, and it dropped the bridge into an uncomfortable silence. Little by little, the sub eased into tractor range of the big white cruiser and, made fast by her magnetic grapples, prepared to transport her patient.

46

The wave of excitement that hit *Hope*'s receiving unit could scarcely be contained. After the long hours of waiting, of speculation, of extrapolation from other odd and beautiful beings among this galaxy alone, the actual sight of *Skipjack* through ports and screens and the knowledge of its rare cargo evoked a stir of emotion, a thrill of the unknown, like a cold breath on the neck, and the people of the *Hope* blew like dust, like dry leaves, in restless gusts of excitement, and eddied around the transporter room, wherein an empty MAX awaited the Elluvon.

Because *Hope* was a hospital ship, the transporter chamber was necessarily large, and the reprogrammed MAX had been placed inside and aerated with methane. It had been suggested at first that *Hope* beam a MAX across into the sub; but since *Skipjack*'s transporter was too small (Marik remembered, with a pang, just how small), they elected to beam the Elluvon directly into the MAX aboard the *Hope*. It would be a tricky operation, because if the coordinates were even a fraction of a degree off, the living Elluvon and the sophisticated metallic apparatus known as a MAX would become a permanent alloy. However, Piet de Mies, *Skipjack*'s senior transporter officer, and Ike Balen, the *wunderkind* of the *Hope*, thought they could do it, and Riker, deliberately shutting out thoughts of his trying to explain an accident to that shifting swarm of alien vessels, gave orders to go ahead.

On an impulse, he added, "Mister Kaplan, ask Mister Marik if they're still coming. He's at the transporter."

Kaplan looked puzzled. "Say again, sir?" He half smiled.

"Just that." He sat back regarding the youngster's handsome, cynical face with something like distaste. Kaplan must have had a terrible case on Mishli, he reflected, for he had been one of the ringleaders in this movement against Marik and at one time had brought Riker a petition, signed by all the junior officers, asking that Marik be swapped back to planetside, or the medical service or anywhere!—except the *Skipjack*. Riker had turned it down abruptly and gave Kaplan no satisfaction, one way or the other, regarding Marik, whom the petition referred to as "this Jonah." The petition was still on file with the records officer. What this boy needs, Riker reflected, is a good, stiff jolt. Nothing as bad as his own shock earlier, but something that Marik could dream up, given time and incentive enough. The captain had no doubt about Kaplan's ability to provide incentive. He sighed, rather pleased with himself. The boy waited with exaggerated tolerance, stopping just short of insolence.

"Ask him," the captain repeated, " 'Are they still coming?' And tell him you'll be accompanying him and Doctor Anderson to the *Hope*." Over his sudden protest, Riker added crisply, *"Now,* mister!"

Kaplan, flushed and angry, snapped "Yessir!" and patched into the lively conversation that was going on between the two ships; he relayed the captain's message curtly and sat in silence to receive the reply. He cut communication abruptly, without a word, and swiveled to face Riker squarely. Arrogantly, Riker decided.

"Answer as follows, sir: 'Affirmative. They are still coming.' There was something else he said—when I told him I'd been ordered to come along. I hope you can understand it. I never bothered to learn gook lingo."

Riker's expression never changed, but his attitude altered subtly, and Kaplan, without moving, seemed to back down.

"In Eisernai, then, Mister Kaplan."

"He said—to you, sir—uh, *'Buchat ge, aton-gne.'* " He looked mystified when Riker grinned broadly, scowled, and wiped the grin away with a firm hand at his chin.

"As you were," Riker muttered, and sat grinning to himself.

Aton-gne, eh? It was the Einai epithet for Erthlikli. *Sun skin. Dago. Nigger. Aton-gne.* Thanks a lot, sun skin, Marik had sent. It was meant in the mood of friendly banter, like the harmless obscenities the Black Gang shouted at one another down in Engineering. It meant nothing unless you wanted to consider friendship. Given that, being called *aton-gne* by your Einai fellow officer meant a lot.

It meant a helluva lot.

Orders were given, switches depressed, and inside *Hope*'s transporter chamber there was a blur of nonform, form, substantiality, and the Elluvon appeared neatly in the MAX, followed first by a flurry of excitement and apprehension among half the accumulated staff and crew, and second—anticlimatically—by Anderson, Marik, and Kaplan, trailing them glumly. As they stepped away, two orderlies swung the MAX out of the chamber, off its wheeled base, and into a hatch in the bulkhead; secured it, programmed a sequence into the Guide, and the MAX was blown on its way to Isolation on a cushion of compressed air.

"Priyam Marik, Doctor Anderson?" The man approaching them in worn hospital fatigues looked like someone's athletic college-age son, with his unruly shock of sandy hair, the careless tan, the sun wrinkles at the corners of his eyes. His smile was at once friendly and appraising. What gave him away were the scars, the twin markings that shone small and white on either side of his throat: the unmistakable imprints of a Krail shock collar. Anderson revised his initial impression—he would have been willing to bet a large sum that there was not a college student in the galaxy—or anyone else, either!—that could bear markings like those and live to tell about it. The only time Marik had seen those marks before, they had been a dark, angry, purple-red—on a jondo, on a slab in the morgue. You did not get a shock collar off and live, too. It was a choice. Either way you lost.

The man extended his hand to Anderson. "Doctor Anderson? I'm Tommy Paige." Behind him the transporter hummed again, and there was a murmur of unease among the dispersing crowd. Paige made an easy *chom-ala* in Marik's direction.

"*Chom-ala,* Priyam. *Tadae samkit zo'on kai tu.*" *God grant your petitions,* or, more literally, *God give you His good ear.* Marik was pleasantly surprised. This Erthlik spoke Eisernai like a mother tongue, and his greeting was in impeccable good taste. He returned the *chom-ala.*

"*A' kai tu,*" he replied. *And to you.*

"If you'd like to come this way," he offered, guiding them through a few knots of chattering staff, "Priyam Sharobi would like to—"

"Freeze!—if you would be so kind," said the clear, imperative voice from the direction of the transporter chamber. Silence fell like a thunderclap, and a few Einai —and one unmistakable Krail—filtered quickly among the staff and held them still and silent with pulse weapons.

"What's the meaning of this?" demanded a heavyset man in his early fifties, Doctor someone, Anderson could not remember his name just off, and Marik had never

49

known it. "What do you call this foolishness?" He pressed his stomach hard against the Krail's pulser, and the tall, thin, pale intruder smiled.

"I call it business," he whispered. "You call it piracy."

"Pirates!" he scoffed, and fell heavily as a short burst from the pulser struck him squarely in the solar plexus.

"Noisy," whispered the very white man. "Very noisy."

"Now," said the imperative voice, "if you will give me your attention, ladies and gentlemen." The crowd's attention swung, as it were one man, toward the transporter chamber and the man who leaned indolently against the doorway.

He was tall for an Einai, lean and flat-muscled, with green-gold skin drawn high over the cheekbones and flat cheeks that disappeared under a full black beard. He had a needler resting lightly in the crook of one arm and a *viith* slung in a leather sleeve behind his shoulder. There was a certain discarded refinement about him and a sense of amusement, as if he were enjoying himself immensely.

"I'd like you all to line up against the walls . . . over there, that's right . . ." He gestured with the needler even as they complied, and his voice had a familiar timbre that reminded Marik of—

"*Kles!*" The word burst from his throat like a shout of surprise, unbeatable as a sneeze.

"What?" asked Anderson numbly. "What? What?"

Kles Mennon's head swiveled, and he saw Marik, let out a wild whoop, vaulted the MAX dolly, picked up a tiny nurse who was in his way, and tossed her to his nearest associate (a huge, slow-moving giant of a man who caught the shrieking girl in both great arms and set her down gently, where she promptly fainted), and grabbed Marik in a great bear hug. He pounded his head and shoulders, laughing through his startlingly white teeth, his eyes squeezed shut so tightly they were wet; and Marik —Anderson stared unbelievingly—cool, aloof Marik, who was always so correct, pounded the pirate's head, too, beat his shoulders, said happy, broken things in Eisernai, and laughed freely. The pirate stepped back and held Marik at arm's length, hugged him again; and Marik pulled free and shook him by the ears, looking at him as if he were trying to memorize his face, drinking in the sight of him.

"I take it you know each other," Anderson ventured, and even Mennon's men grinned at that. Mennon glanced at him.

"This is my brother," he said, and then corrected himself and said intensely, as if he reveled in it, "This is my *lord!*" Marik, evidently deciding that a change of subject was in order, and to cover any embarrassment, he made tardy introductions.

"Kles, this is Doctor Anderson. Doctor Paige. Neal, this is Kles Mennon. We were raised together."

"We've met," Paige said. "The rain forest beyond Bex-Elakli."

Recognition lit Mennon's face. *"Duli.* So the Krail didn't get you after all." Paige had no desire to enlighten him, but the sharp yellow eyes took in the scars and lines. "Or maybe they did. Anyway, you're in good company." He rapped Marik on the head with his knuckles. "Very good company." He gestured at Paige carelessly.

"This *duli,* here, took care of my side when I ditched the *Tsai* in the jungle. Only Ilai and Jek were with me. I would have died if he hadn't gotten me to the Erthlik ship —where I found you."

"They told me the *Pacific* had been scuttled," Marik said quietly. "I thought you went down with her."

"No, it was the other way. When I woke the next morning, they'd taken you away. No one would tell me anything. A Krail officer finally told me you had died."

"I lived," Marik whispered, seeing on his face how it had been for him. "Kles, he knew—he had to know!—I lived!"

"But he swore!" His face twisted so that it was hard to tell whether he wanted to laugh or cry, and he made a short, explosive burst of sound. It could not have been called laughter.

"So—the next morning—I scuttled the ship!—with everyone aboard!—except the Krail who helped me fight my way free. For you, Dao! I did it for you!—for vengeance!"

Marik regarded him with something akin to horror. "No! Kles!—you had no right!—to impose that burden on me! Those *people*—"

The pirate interrupted him, half angry, half entreating. "My lord Eisernon, you were worth it, don't you see?

51

Erthlikli—for Einai!—And an Erthlik ship! For *Eisernon!*"
His hands clenched the air and held it. "Your ancestors
would have understood—and approved!"

He dropped into Eisernai in his impassioned defense,
not realizing that Paige, who was listening interestedly,
although he pretended to study the faces around him with
bored tolerance, was casually easing his way toward the
wall hatch. There was a setting on the guide that if seen
by the pirates and recognized for what it was, would make
the *Hope* as expendable, in the pirate's opinion, as the
Pacific had been.

Eisernon, Mennon had called the new Priyam. Strange,
to call a man by the name of an empire. Of course, he
mused, edging past a tight knot of captive staff with an
absent, apologetic smile, Henry the Eighth had referred to
himself as "we" because, in effect, he *was* England. Caesar
had called Cleopatra "Egypt." He searched his memory.
Could this Marik be akin to the imperial Mariks? The
ancient line of emperors? That would account for his
being Han—and for Mennon's unaccountable devotion to
him. But—a Han? Serving aboard a Federation sub like a
common sailor? It was hard to believe. More than that, it
was doubtful to the point of being preposterous.

He moved closer to the hatch and halted when he
caught the eye of an orderly, who figured out what he was
up to and started making his way through the crowd in
that direction, too. Both of them were trying to reach the
guide, which was set at *unlock*. As long as it remained in
that position, a simple sequence could recall the Elluvon's
MAX. That must not happen. There could only be one
reason for the pirate's presence here: An emissary from
another galaxy had to have a certain economic value to
the wolves of this one. Someone—the Krail, Paige was
willing to bet—would undoubtedly pay them well for it.
They could not be allowed to gain possession of the fragile
Elluvon. Paige meant to see to it that they did not.

The guide stood at *Unlock*, a mere ten feet away. But
those ten feet were not crowded two and three deep with
people. It was a nasty, open space to have to cross, in the
face of men with needlers and *viith*. He paused, feeling
eyes on his back, and turned naturally, slowly, to meet the
expressionless ice-blue eyes of the Krail henchman. Paige
suppressed a shiver. He had been a slave of these people

52

and knew very well what that frozen smile could mean. He decided to wait.

The Einai were still talking in those low tones, the pirate trying to explain, the Priyam implacable in his terrible determination that his life had not been worth the loss of the hospital ship.

"The guilt is solely yours, Kles," was saying. And then, in Erthenglish, "You have changed, risTadae."

"And have you," Mennon answered slowly, the yellow eyes cloudy as he took in the Federation uniform, the medical insignia, both Federation and Einai, at Marik's throat. "So you've joined them."

"Yes, I've joined them."

"After Sum ChiT'ath, how could you do it?"

"After Sum ChiT'ath," Marik rejoined soberly, "what else was left?"

"There was Mishli," Mennon said crisply. "There was the baby."

Marik's eyes narrowed until they were bright grey lines. "What baby? What are you talking about?"

Mennon looked interested. "You really don't know, do you?" He smiled one of his quick, white smiles. "I think I'll leave it to Mishli to tell you. I don't want to spoil her surprise."

Parry Kaplan snorted. "Talk about surprises—" he began, but Anderson took the pipe out of his mouth and cleared his throat.

"Mister Mennon, this is all well and good, but these people have jobs to do. This piracy game is wearing a little thin, don't you think?"

"I think it's ridiculous!" Parry Kaplan announced. "This clown can't come in here and—" But the small man with the shaved head warned him to silence with a wicked-looking viith, and he subsided sullenly.

"No game, unfortunately," Mennon told Anderson with a shrug. "It seems that I am now persona non grata among the Erthlikli because of the Pacific incident"—(Marik winced)—"and among the Krail I am unwelcome, too, because of a slight indiscretion regarding the destruction of one of their strongholds. And among our own people, Dao," the white teeth flashed quickly, "I need only tell you that the Klan is active again. You'll want to be careful of that. That leaves only space, and the poor man lives as he can. As he must." He shifted the needler to his underarm and brought the muzzle to bear on Marik.

"Dao," he said gently, with a tinge of regret, "we've come for the Elluvon." Marik fixed him with that level grey gaze.

"Through me," he said.

Mennon looked embarrassed, then smiled charmingly and spread his hands. "My lord, I have you at the point of a gun. Be reasonable. Give me the beast. I promise you I won't hurt it. I would not hurt it; it's valuable to me. The Krail will pay me a great deal of money for it."

Paige risked another glance at the guide, eight feet away. The Einai giant was watching him constantly now; no chance to slip over there unseen. He waited. As soon as the two started in again—

"You're wasting vital time, Kles," Marik was saying. "The Elluvon is badly in need of our help. There are forces here you can't begin to grasp."

"I'll take that risk. I mean to have it, Dao."

Marik stood deceptively casual before him. Anderson was not fooled by it. He had stood just that way minutes before he killed a corrupt Federation delegate in hand-to-hand combat.

"I think not, *risTadae*," he said softly.

Paige had time only to hit the *lock* switch before the butt of the giant's needler struck him down. Before he hit the deck, the others had forced the murmuring, excited members of the staff back to their places against the wall. The doctor who had been hit originally was beginning to stir and retch, and solicitous hands helped prop him against a metal supporting member.

Mennon drew his *viith* and gestured with it at the orderly. "How do you unlock this thing?" The man was frightened, but he stood his ground stolidly.

"I don't know. I'm just an orderly. I clean up, that's all."

Mennon studied his face for an instant longer and murmured, "Not likely." He placed his hand flat against the guide studs and activated many conflicting commands at once.

At this the automatic systems cut in, and with a command overload, they shut the facility down. Somewhere, deep in the maze of tangled metallic spaghetti that constituted the ship's MAX-transit system, the MAX containing the Elluvon slowed perceptibly. The shutdown had effectively cut off the pressure-relay system that sped the MAX along, and without it, without sufficient velocity, the heavy metal cylinder bumped roughly a few times, grated unevenly along the bottom and sides of the tube, slewed around wildly, and wedged itself tightly into a curve built with proper velocity and pressure in mind, and therefore with only fractions of centimeters to spare. This wild careening cylinder, gone out of control, stuck fast in the curve, its occupant hanging at an uncomfortable forty-five-degree angle to the horizontal and a thirty-degree angle, head downward, to the perpendicular. It was quiet down there. It was very dark. And the Elluvon was alone. Never, never in its life had it been alone before, either mentally or physically. It was frightened beyond all telling and too weak even to think loudly for help. Now, faced with a situation it had never encountered and having no precedent to refer to, it took what seemed to it the only reasonable action.

It began to die.

In space, beyond sight of the linked vessels, the gyrating blue globes took on another, newer configuration and paused in their forward passage. They waited.

No sooner had Mennon's hand hit the guide than Marik slammed it free, but it was too late. He punched a few sequences and got no response, Mennon's *viith* pricking the skin over his ribs.

"Don't try me too far, Dao," Mennon laughed, lightly, dangerously.

Marik, ignoring him, switched off the guide to prevent further damage.

"It's jammed. The whole system's shut down. We'll have to go in after it." To the orderly, "Where's your nearest emergency access?"

"Down here, sir, but—you're not going to be able to get in there with that leg. There are places down there where you have to hang on with both hands and legs just to survive. Some of those verticals are over a thousand feet straight down."

"Then you go and get it out," Mennon suggested gently. The man shook his head vehemently.

"No, sir," he said. "No, sir, you want to kill me, well,

you just kill me here, but I'm not going down there. Nothing in my contract says I gotta go down the tubes for no alien. Not me, boy. Uh, uh."

Parry Kaplan stepped forward, brushing a needler aside in a rather melodramatic gesture. "I'll go." Mennon regarded him with pity and amusement, then sleeved his *viith*.

"Oh, Chu'l T'ath!" he moaned. "Look what we have here. A living, breathing hero." Some of Mennon's cutthroats and even some of the staff smiled at that because he was so young and had such an appealing face, and because it was the kind of a thing a young man could be expected to do; but he thought they were laughing at him, and he could not stand that.

"Maybe I'm no hero," he snapped, face flushed and eyes blazing, "but I wouldn't sacrifice my wife's life to save my own skin!"

Marik's face paled to a clear, even gold, the color of Erthlik skin, with no tinge of green apparent anywhere, and Mennon looked at him, amused and uncomprehending.

"What's he talking about, Dao?" A thought hit him, and he shook his head, ever so slightly, as if to negate whatever terrible idea had come to him. "No. Not you, Dao. *Not Mishli!*"

"Ask him," taunted Kaplan. "Ask this coward, this— this *Jonah!*—where she is!" Mennon whirled on Marik, caught him by the sides of the head, by his hands against his face, like a brother would search the face of a brother for signs of life and see no life there. Marik said nothing, only watched him with those steady grey eyes, asking nothing, revealing nothing except by his terrible pallor.

"For the love of T'ath," Mennon shouted, *"where is she?"* Kaplan, halfway lowered into the access hatch, waited to hear the answer. He was openly, frankly gloating, and Anderson could have cheerfully wrung his neck. Marik seemed to have aged ten years in the few moments since Kaplan reopened the wound. His voice, when it came, was steady and even, but it lacked strength, as though some inner rent was bleeding where no one could see, and sapping his vigor.

"I let her die," he said quietly.

Mennon's face changed; it underwent a transformation

even as they watched. The skin appeared to tighten across the harsh planes of bone, and the yellow eyes slitted in disbelief. A wet white line of teeth showed in an incredulous grimace, a travesty of a smile. He repeated Marik's words silently to himself. He must have stared at Marik a full ten seconds, trying to read his face, his eyes, his tightly locked thoughts; then Mennon made a great sound, a roar, like a wounded animal and struck with his open hand. It made a loud *pop*, like a pistol shot, and left the imprint of his hand in livid green welts on his cheek. Marik did nothing; he just stood there, bemused and vulnerable. The second time, and the third time, and the fourth, Mennon hit him with his interlocked fists, the face first, then the neck, and then the face again. When he fell forward onto his hands and knees, he kicked him. He kept making that wordless roar, like a madman, and Marik, while he began to dodge the worst blows as best he could, refused to fight back.

Kaplan, with a grim satisfaction, sank below sight into the tube, and Anderson tried to speak out in Marik's defense, but the man with the shaved head pushed the muzzle of his needler against his teeth, and he jerked away from it and watched the kill. There was no other way to think of it: It was as one-sided as it could conceivably be. Marik was taking a brutal punishment and doing nothing— absolutely nothing—to defend himself. He peered over heads and saw that Marik had regained his feet, and Mennon, burning brightly as a tiger, had drawn his *viith*.

"Kles," Marik begged softly, "don't make me fight you." And the pirate laughed harshly, knowing the Han could kill with their minds. He poked his bushy head with stiff fingers as he talked.

"You can't, my *lord*." He spat it like an epithet. "Remember? Not with *that!* Ethics, remember?" He came forward, crouched and weaving, the *viith* moving in eager little jerks in his hand. Marik did not move. He watched him with a great sadness, a grief, in his face. His mouth was bleeding, and a swollen purple bruise distorted one cheekbone, but his grief was not for himself.

"I don't want to fight you, Kles, *risTadae*."

The shaggy head snapped up. "Never call me that!" he snarled. "Never call me 'brother' again!" He made that wordless cry once more and leaped at him feet first, aiming for the chest, the *viith* poised for the kill. Marik's quick dodge sidestepped the lethal stab and caught it as a burning swipe down the length of his upper arm. He slapped it and wheeled to parry another stab but caught the brunt of a second flying kick right above the kidneys; he retained his footing blindly, only dimly seeing Kles leaping at him yet again. He avoided the thrust an instant too late, and the *viith* caught him, slashing his defensive forearm, missing his throat. He fell back, eluding his aggressor, shying off. It was clear that he had no intention of fighting back. It became painful to watch. People began to turn their heads away.

Mennon was at him again, in no hurry now, pressing his advantage. It was swipe, jab, nothing fatal yet. Mennon was too skilled for that, but Marik's uniform was in soggy ribbons, and it was getting hard for him to avoid that *viith*, pressed back as he was, time and time again, among the crowded staff against the wall. He was bleeding freely.

"Get those people out of here!" he ordered thickly, and even Mennon, at his men's quick inquiring glance, nodded shortly and fell back a few steps. The staff bumbled noisily out, pushing and chattering, but Anderson shoved his way past them.

"It wasn't like he told you, you damn' fool," he yelled. "He didn't—" The needler butt caught him slightly above and behind the left ear, and the giant dragged him out into the corridor with the others. In the ensuing melee, the orderly slipped away unseen, hurried to the nearest wall communicator, and called Security.

Green drops hit the deck slowly and reminded Marik foggily of the melancholy autumn rains, put him in mind of the end of something, he could not remember what. He tried to drag himself up from his hands and knees, but Kles kicked him down and landed a nasty gash across his back. He was in earnest now, and even as Marik rolled free and gained his footing once again, he saw that Mennon meant to kill him.

Kles had always reacted with that rage, that ungovernable rage, when he felt helpless or bereft. Always before it had burned itself out, in very few moments, doing no damage. Now Marik saw that even his own blood was

58

not going to quench it. He regretted what he was going to have to do.

"One last time, Kles," he entreated huskily. "Don't make me fight you." Mennon's lip curled in contempt.

"The boy was right, *umbin*," he spat. "You *are* a coward."

He lifted the *viith* for the coup de grace, but the arm never came down. Marik's clenched fist gripped it in midair and gave it a curious little wrench, and he heard the bones snap—and then felt them—even as Marik's left hand caught his beard, jerked it upward, and the right hand snatched the *viith* and drew a thin, shallow, harmless line around the throat from ear to ear. Marik switched the *viith* to his left hand and slapped Mennon's stunned face, back and forth, rocking his head until the yellow eyes cleared and some sanity returned to them with the grief.

"The baby," he demanded intensely, and when Mennon stared numbly at him, making no answer, he repeated, "The baby, Kles! Mishli's baby!—and mine! Where is it?"

Mennon took a deep breath and closed his eyes. "Raintree Street."

There were heavy, running footsteps in the corridor, and Marik stumbled over to the transporter chamber and activated the controls.

"You came across last," he muttered thickly. "They'll still be set for your ship." Mennon stood staring at him stupidly, like a man awaking from a bad dream. "Go!" Marik shouted suddenly, savagely. "Do you want them to catch you?"

Mennon, cradling his broken arm against his body, trotted after the others into the chamber. Just as he reached the portal, Marik stopped him.

"Kles!" It crackled like ice. Mennon whirled, and Marik threw the *viith* to him, still stained with his blood. "Something to remember me by," he said.

Mennon caught it clumsily in his left hand and cut himself, just as the security men pounded through the portal. He stared at it, then at Marik.

"I'll remember you," he promised grimly. He made a strange, violent mark with his cut hand on the access, and then he stepped into the chamber and was gone.

Marik shut off the control and leaned heavily on both hands, his head bent over the console. He wished that he could weep. He wished Kles had not drawn that particular symbol, most especially not in blood. The blood make it final. Even when he closed his eyes, he could see it there, green and irrevocable.

It was the symbol for enmity.

Chapter IV

In the books it was always referred to in the singular, as the Tube, but in reality it was a network of tubes, a veritable circulatory system of tubes, that lay close under the ship's skin and serviced her many nerve centers. The books might refer to them as they liked; to the engineers, the technicians, the Science Officers, and the crews whose job it was to keep them free of even the merest fleck of dust, the intricate lacery of metal conduits was known as the tubes, plural, and the danger of working in them was an historical fact. Even in the earliest days of space travel, *Encyclopedia Galactica* reported pedantically the expression "going down the tubes" was synonymous with extermination. They knew. You could not argue with history, most especially if you were familiar with the tubes.

It was not as dangerous now as it had been in the beginning. Down in engineering, Kaplan knew, there was a device that displayed the entire webwork of tubes (sort of a three-dimensional holographic grid, he guessed) and with it the engineers could pinpoint trouble, or potential trouble, in any given tube at any given time. It was a vital piece of instrumentation, for among other things it prevented a MAX being shunted into a segment containing, say, a maintenance crew; or a volunteer crawling around in the dark looking for some dumb alien that would probably turn out to be an oversized bug, anyway.

Kaplan knew a great deal about it. Like everyone who had read several books on MAX-transit systems, he felt familiar with their operation. What he did not know, and what no book had bothered to elucidate upon, was what happened to the wonderful system when its computer went down. Then it was different. Then you were not sitting comfortably in the academy library, reading about it, you were right there; and the discrepancy between the book's literary objectivity and the burning of space-cold metal through your uniform trousers was painfully evident.

And then there was the darkness. He had not expected the darkness.

The tubes were dark. They were lonely and cold and very, very dark, and Kaplan had expected the aloneness and the cold and even the little finger of excitement working in his belly that he might have taken for fear if he didn't know better; but he was unprepared for the darkness. The books always said the tubes were well lighted, and so they always were except, of course, during a shutdown. Like now. When the light was needed most. He swallowed and scrambled on a few feet further, his tool belt clanking hollowly.

It was going to be hard to find the Elluvon in the dark. It would be harder still to avoid the open vertical shafts the orderly had warned them about. He had a powerful torch and a tool belt that someone had handed him at the last minute, but he found that just bracing himself against the steep slope and curving sidewalls kept both hands too busy to bother with tools. His boots had a disconcerting tendency to slip out from under him, sending him into short, uncontrollable slides, and he finally sat cautiously and scooted along on his heels and seat, which was a less precipitate, if not quite as heroic, form of locomotion.

He regretted his having refused the communicator they had wanted him to have, but at the time he had been more interested in seeing Marik get what was due him. He never thought of the second officer as "Mister Marik," but as "Marik," the way you called an animal by a one-word name. Not all Einai were animals, though. *She* had not been an animal, with her uptilted brows and her delicate hands and the way her lashes touched her cheeks and made a man go fidgety inside. *She* had been a real, honest-to-God woman; it was Marik who was the animal. Damn Marik, anyway!—letting her die like that.

He wondered briefly whether the pirate had killed him. Probably so; it was unlikely that Mennon, having grasped the offensive, would cuff Marik around and then decide to walk away friends. No, he had been armed and enraged. There was not much chance that Marik, vulnerable as he was, could have survived. Personally, Kaplan hoped for the worst. It would serve him right if Mennon had chopped him into little pieces!—for Marik's imaginary dragons to gobble up! And, he reflected, *Skipjack* would probably breathe a collective sigh of relief if he had.

Sliding along absently in the dark, his thoughts thus occupied, Kaplan suddenly froze with fright as his right foot slipped abruptly over a curved edge and into an unseen abyss, his left foot following quickly and the rest of him threatening to plunge along right after it. The metal was so smooth, so slick, that before he half realized what was happening, his legs had slid into the yawning invisible pit almost up to the hips, past his point of no return. With an instinct born of terror, he flipped over on his stomach in a frantic lunge and caught himself on his hands, fingers widely spread, and hung there balanced for a precarious, heart-pounding moment over the blind emptiness of the abyss. Even his cheek, pressed desperately against the metal, provided a small friction coefficient to support him, and just for an instant he had a wild, unreasonable hope that he would be able to pull himself to safety; but at that moment, the ship gave a gargantuan shrug, a sharp thump, a sudden roll, as though it had been hit by something so vast and powerful that the immense bulk of the starcruiser could be pitched and rolled by the stroke of a powerful fluke. Far in the distance, collision bells rang hysterically, drowning out his cry.

Parry Kaplan had just enough time before he hit the hard, unyielding metal at the bottom of the shaft to realize what it was that had struck the ship. Then there was the sickening jolt of impact, and neither dragons, nor Marik, nor anything else, mattered anymore.

"*Hope*'s under attack, Paul!" The forward screen flashed

to life as MBenga wheeled at his station, but before Riker could make a reply, the shock hit *Skipjack*, throwing Jen out of her chair and knocking Hayashi, who had been on the bridge to collect a bet, against his console, where he swore softly in Japanese. Riker hit the collision alarm. "Where're we hit?"

There on the screen the *Hope* sustained yet another blow from the impossible creatures that sported and curvetted about it, and the mammoth hull rolled majestically and righted itself as slowly.

"Starboard frames ninety-two, three, and four. Two looks pretty bad."

"Get on it. Jen, open a channel to *Hope*," he ordered shortly, "and nix that thing, will you?" He gestured at the collision alarm.

Her stilted reply was lost under the bone-rattling impact of a direct hit by the cavorting creatures around them, and little metal voices whispered and chittered over the com, reading out damage reports and requesting information.

"Are the shields holding?" Riker demanded, and MBenga nodded quickly and continued his checkout of the ship, compartment by compartment, as the screen changed and the image of *Hope*'s captain, one Donelang Kris, appeared on it. Captain Kris was a thin, quiet, dignified Xhole of middle years whose wrinkled blue skin and serene countenance belied the brilliant talent for organization and leadership that lay under the delicate skull. He bowed.

"I am honored, Captain," he offered, and Riker returned a perfunctory bow from where he sat.

"The honor is mine, sir." He meant it. Not only the honor, but the awkwardness of speaking face to face with the man the fleet called the Blue Death. It was hard to believe that the tranquil countenance before him belonged to the man responsible for the destruction of over one-third of the ships in earth's third fleet, during the One Day War of the Han, when an earthling destroyer had mercilessly fired upon his hospital ship. Because he carried no weaponry, he used his vessel, a twisted hulk filled with the dead and dying, as a lure, a dare, a ram, and taunted the Erthlik captains into fatal mistakes. Emotions were running high then, and earth paid dearly for them.

Afterward, when the carnage was done, the squad of marines that found him, seared and broken at the helm, beamed him down to the morgue with a black tag on his foot. A young Priyam named Mykar Sharobi discovered their mistake and thereby resuscitated the man whom the navy would most like to have seen dead, right about then. Kris had done a most terrible damage, and earth never forgot it.

Neither did Xholemeache.

The pacific Xhole could not coutenance willful killing on any terms, no matter what the provocation. When Donelang Kris got home, he found there was no home. His house had been carefully disassembled; no stone lay upon another, and his glades had been uprooted, the soil neatly repacked into the turf. His animals were gone. His wife did not recognize him, nor would she. No one would speak his name. It was not as if he was dead. It was as though he had never existed.

The court-martial was as long as it was sensational. The verdict was unanimous: temporary insanity. Battle fatigue. There were psychiatrists. There was a rest home on a peaceful planet. Kris was sane, and everybody knew he was sane, but it was either a rest home or a lynch mob. He accepted their decision obediently. When at last the furor had died down, and he returned to base headquarters for his orders, he found he had been assigned to captain the U.S.S. *Hope*, which at that time was a globular old tub where we sent misfits—to be well rid of them. He accepted that blow impassively with all the rest and after a time came to identify with her age and infirmities.

Many years later, when Sharobi took over as chief and went around with long legs and a dark scowl, tossing out incompetents and selecting the galaxy's choice personnel for his big, shiny new starcruiser that made everything else in the fleet look pretty much like a rowboat, the first man he requested—and would not be convinced otherwise—was Captain Donelang Kris, the Blue Death.

Another small shudder snapped Riker back from his deliberation, and he got down to business. "My ship is being attacked by an unknown enemy, sir. I don't know how long we can hold out. I suggest we terminate rendezvous and schedule linkup in another sector."

Kris started to answer when a violent collision rocked his bridge. He said something quickly in the clicking syllables of his own tongue to someone off screen and then resumed his decorum.

"Pardon. Let me enlighten our situation. Our ships are positioned squarely in the path of the Migration of the dragons. It is somewhat similar, I believe, to your walk for elephants. Every year, during their stars' revolution around its binary, they migrate. The star has revolved; therefore, they are migrating."

"You knew this—sir—even when you agreed to rendezvous?"

"Affirmative, Captain," the wrinkled blue man assented quickly. "You have aboard your ship an Einai officer, have you not? I understand that some few of that race are familiar with the dragons. We had hoped that the transfer would take place before the herd reached these coordinates."

Two more sudden shocks rocked the *Skipjack*, and *Hope* must also have been buffeted, for the screen swung wildly before centering again on Kris's impassive face. "Most unfortunate," he added placidly, "that it did not."

"We have plotted coordinates for the new rendezvous. I can have them patched in to your computer immediately."

Kris made an odd offhand gesture, as if throwing away something small. His suggestion, probably, Riker thought. "Most embarrassingly," he articulated clearly, "neither of us is able to leave."

Riker eyed him balefully. "Say again, Captain," he said flatly.

"The nature of the dragons is such," the blue man informed him, "that the negative charge generated by our passage would be equivalent to bait. Then they would surely destroy us."

"Throwing out blood," Riker speculated, "to drive away sharks."

"Possibly." Kris's tone indicated how little his ignorance of the word "shark" meant to him. "In any case, Captain Riker, we are trapped here until the herd chooses to continue its migration."

"And that'll probably take some time."

"It is a large herd and we are a new experience for it."

"Is there any way to dispose of them? Drive them off,

kill them?" The blue man's expression grew somber, and it was a long moment before he spoke. His voice was chill.

"These creatures, Captain Riker, are a protected species. My people, the Xhole, have been preserving and studying them for the past millennium. They are matter on the verge of becoming energy—or energy metamorphosing into matter. Our interest in them has gone beyond a federation project, sir. It has become a planetary religion. We are observing creation taking place! You will not disturb it, please."

Riker was taken aback and hastened to apologize. He had not, he explained, understood, being a member of a young and thoughtless people. He summarily withdrew the suggestion. He would do no harm to the dragons, and he hoped, in turn, that the ships could get away with little or no harm done to them. Donelang Kris replied curtly that the survival of the ships would probably depend largely upon the skill and good judgment of their officers and rang off with polite best wishes for the captain's continued good health. Riker sat back slowly, smarting like a small boy who had been soundly spanked. He blew out his breath in a silent whistle, hoping fervently that the absent members of his crew were doing a bit better than those aboard the *Skipjack*.

He stared at the forward screen for a thoughtful moment, tapping the control studs absently with the edge of his hand, and squinted at the image through narrowed eyes. "Jen," he mused at last, "get me a channel to Com-Fleet."

Tommy Paige put down the portable hand suture and stretched a plastex and gauze tape across the stitched gash on Marik's arm.

"That about does it, I think," he said, and as Marik murmured his thanks, the nurse who had been swabbing the cuts on his chest and ribs straightened up, bringing her into close proximity with the handsome alien, so close, in fact, that he could smell the fresh scent of her skin and the trace of musk in her hair. She knew it and smiled warmly at him, and he watched her with sober interest in those brooding grey eyes of his.

"Did you want to stitch these, too, Doctor?" Her voice was clear and confident. "Some of them are pretty deep."

She started gathering up soiled sponges in a steel pan, waiting around, making work.

Paige looked at them closely, spread the edges of some of them apart to see how deep they were, ran a thin line of surgical epoxy along the worst of them, and flattened it with his thumb in three or four firm swipes. "That ought to take care of it. How do you feel, Priyam."

Marik squinted at him over his puffy cheekbone and smiled cautiously, holding his bruised, split lips with a careful hand. "Wonderful," he mumbled. He felt gingerly of his cut arm and winced a bit as it pulled, stiffening. "Just wonderful." He reached for the clean tunic they had found him and began tugging it over his head.

"We ought to admit you, you know," Paige continued. "Make sure you don't have any internal injuries."

"If I have, *Duli* Paige," he told him dryly, "you'll be the first to know." He fastened his belt and began clipping his communicator and his usual instruments to it. Reluctantly, there being no more work for her, the nurse left.

Paige pushed that shock of unruly hair off his forehead and paused for a moment. "If you don't mind, Priyam," he ventured, "I haven't been a jungle *duli* for some time."

Marik flushed. "If you prefer, sir," he said stiffly, "I will address you as 'doctor.'"

"What I would prefer, sir," Paige retorted hotly, "is for you to call me Tom—just that!—Tom!"

Marik finished with the instruments. "It is not our custom," he answered shortly.

"Suit yourself." Paige, stung, crossed to where the coffee urn stood on a cluttered table of its own, there in the corner, and poured himself a cup of coffee. That's what you get, he fumed, trying to offer friendship indiscriminately nowadays. Give a guy a hand up and you pull back a bloody stump. To hell with it, then! If the remote Priyam Marik wanted to sit—and brood—in his ivory tower (coming down, occasionally, for unilateral duels with some pretty rough playmates, who summarily beat him to a pulp), that was no skin off Tom Paige's nose. It was not as if old Tom was hard up for friends. If the truth were known, and he was not sure it was not, it was the high and mighty Priyam Marik who seemed to come up short in that direction. When your own subordinates would sell you down river, and your best friend delivered

68

a knife lecture on how not to kill a wife, it seemed reasonable that you could use a friend or two. Not that Paige gave a damn! Let the fellow sit!—and rot!—if he had a mind to. To hell with him!

He turned around, the coffee cup still in his hand, to say as much, but there was an expression on Marik's face that struck him dumb, an expression of such anguish and vulnerability, of needing his friendship and being unable to accept it, that Paige impulsively thrust the coffee container at him. After a moment's hesitation, Marik accepted the cup and nodded. "Tom," he said, by way of thanks. Paige pulled a slow grin and poured himself another cup, and Marik, careful of his sore mouth, began to grin, too, when suddenly they were thrown completely off their feet by the ship's sudden rolling. Paige fell against Marik, who was knocked backward into the examining table, grunting softly in agony as his bruised back struck it squarely. Hot coffee splashed both of them, and they fetched up against the far wall as the ship recovered. Emergency warnings, muted here, *bonged* softly.

"What the hell was that?" Paige demanded, and Marik passed a hand across his eyes as if to clear them.

"I'd forgotten," he said to himself, and then, to Paige, "It's the dragons. Here there are dragons."

The wall communicator signaled, and Paige hit it. "Emergency. Paige." He scowled unbelievingly at the alien. *Dragons?*

"Mister Marik to the power deck," piped the bridge.

"Right. Any news on Priyam Sharobi?" Paige wanted to know, and the communicator chuckled metallically.

Priyam Sharobi, it confided, was in OR M-13, the morgue, doing an autopsy on one of the Elluvon cadavers. Since all ORs were on the cleverly engineered equivalent of gymbals, he had not noticed the shocks at all. When a resident came in to inform him of them, Sharobi had had him reposition a badly placed light at precisely the correct angle and then had preoccupiedly invited him to get out. It was the general consensus that crusty old Sharobi could take care of himself. The communicator repeated the message that Mister Marik was urgently needed in Engineering, down on the power deck, and rang off.

"Coming?" Marik queried over his shoulder as he set out, and Paige obligingly caught up to him, matching his long, easy stride to Marik's noticeable limp. Two women doctors nodded pleasantly at them as they passed and turned to smile and murmur between themselves. When they reached the lift, Paige asked, "What's this 'Mister Marik' stuff? Don't they know you're a Priyam? Or did I miss something—somewhere along the line?"

Marik shook his head. No, he said, Paige had not missed anything. He would tell him about it—sometime—provided he really wanted to know.

The lift admitted them and sped along. There were three other people in the conveyance with them: two internes, who were discussing the Elluvon's scutes as if they had invented them, and the nurse Marik had seen earlier.

"You turn up just everywhere, don't you, Priyam?" she said brightly, and Marik was spared the necessity for answering her by a second and a quick third shock that caused the lift to jounce precariously in its passage. The lights flickered and dimmed, then came on strongly again, pretending nothing had happened, and the doors slid open at the morgue to let the internes out and again, only a moment away, at Central Supply, where the nurse left them. She turned as she got out and lifted a hand awkwardly.

"Bye," she said hopefully, smiling at Marik, and the doors cut her image off as suddenly as closing the eyes. Under the subdued hum of the motors, Paige whistled quietly to himself and wagged his head.

"Got to beat 'em off with a stick," he muttered, grinning.

Marik looked at him. "I beg your pardon?"

"The women. The nurses, the techs, the honeymeds." He shoved both hands in the pockets of his fatigues and studied the overhead with admiring interest. "Let ol' tall, dark, and feline hit the wards, and—zap!" He lifted a hand with great deliberation and snapped his fingers. "Never had a chance."

"You are losing your mind," Marik informed him complacently.

As the lift stopped and whispered open for them at Engineering, a female tech looked up from her console and lifted a brow with interest. Marik flushed and ignored her, and Paige only grinned again and snapped his fingers.

The engineers, immaculate in their white fatigues with the symbol of the *Hope*, an anchor surrounded by twelve stars worked at the left breast, were gathered around a display grid of the tube system. While Marik had a working familiarity with tube systems (it was his custom to inspect *Skipjack*'s tubes regularly), the sub carried only emergency sleds, mere covered conveyances, which were smaller and less complex than MAXs and required tubes that were shorter, less highly pressurized and smaller in diameter than these aboard *Hope*. Marik's inspections were customarily carried out in felt shoes and sweat suit, inching along on his belly so as not to smash his head against the overhead; according to the display before him, a man could actually walk—crouched over, to be sure, but walk!—in *Hope*'s yawning, high-pressure courses.

One of the engineers got to his feet as they approached. He was a short, stocky Erthlik with iron-grey hair and a curious quirk at one corner of his mouth. "Mister Marik, I'm Les Berrey." They shook hands briefly, and he made an offhand gesture at the others. "This is Greco, Ragusa, Collins, Connelly, and Ory. Diamond's back there somewhere, I don't know." They made assenting noises, lifted a hand, nodded, as Berrey continued. "We've got a problem. The tubes have been shut down from one of the master stations—"

"The transporter room," Marik assisted, and Berrey's mouth quirked, making a hard line.

"Huh! That just about ties it! We can't override Transport. See here . . ." He indicated a tube segment where there was a dark, cylindrical mass hanging askew in a curve. "That's your Elluvon. Stuck fast. We could get it out easy by shoving another MAX through there. Let the pressure 'float' it out. But some clown decided to crawl in and try to wrestle a half-ton MAX out by hand. Here he is, down here . . ." He pointed at a vertical shaft, some distance away from the grounded MAX, at the bottom of which lay an inert mass, roughly man shaped.

"Do you have a life glow on him?" Marik wanted to know, and Berrey nodded.

"Oh, sure. That's the problem. If he'd broken his neck, we wouldn't mind sending the MAX in and no sweat about pressure buildup. But with him alive in there, we can't make a move.

"And there's another thing, Mister Marik." His mouth made that hard, tight quirk that Marik was beginning to understand was indicative of tension. "The captain just let us know that there's an alien armada hanging out in space a couple of years out. They're close enough to be visible on the screens. Captain Kris thinks they have something to do with your Elluvon bug. That puts us in a tight spot. If we save the alien, we kill your man. I'm not prepared to do that. If we go in after the hero, the alien's going to die down there, and then we'll have that armada down our necks. I'm not ready for that, either. We're between a rock and a hard place."

"You've talked to the bridge." It was a quiet statement of fact, not a question at all. Berrey inclined his head heavily, lips pursed.

"Both of them. They keep trying to reach ComFleet, but so far, no joy. So it's up to you. You're the science officer, and you're here. Ordinarily *our* SO would make the decision, but he came down with jungle fever, off of Sauvage, and it took him out. Looks like you're elected. Whatever you say goes." The men shifted uncomfortably, and Ragusa lit a cigarette. Greco gave him a surreptitious elbow, and he muttered, "Oh, sorry," and put it out. The rest of the Black Gang looked at him in disgust. It was common knowledge that Einai reacted to tobacco the way Earthlings reacted to heroin. They could not afford that, right now. They needed Marik at his keenest.

Marik stepped closer to the flickering grid, Connelly and Ory moving aside to give him more room. Taking a stylus, he carefully traced the Elluvons' probable path from Transport to the site of the accident. He repeated the process with Kaplan's passage, and he could see where and how he had fallen. A vertical shaft—he pulled an instrument off his belt and measured—perhaps twenty or twenty-five feet deep, branched off the main course just abaft one of the automatic valves that controlled air flow. When the tubes were idle, the circular metal shunts were open to prevent accidents concerning vacuums and collapses; when a MAX (or multiple MAXs) were being sent through, they snicked shut automatically to provide a separate air stream for each MAX and to prevent exactly what had happened in this instance: the grounding of a half-ton metal cylinder, carrying an injured or ill patient, and its subsequent stranding down in the labyrinths of metal, miles—and inches—from help.

"Incidentally," Marik offered, absorbed in tracing the shortest route between himself and the tube where Kaplan lay injured. "Mister Kaplan volunteered to go down the tubes at my express opinion that we had to be physically present to rescue the Elluvon."

The engineers started talking all at once then, trying to ask how he expected to haul a half ton of MAX out of there on his back, and whether he was not familiar, as their SO had been, with proper tubes operations, and why the simple expedient of shunting another MAX through would not slide the first one along neatly on its flotation cushion of compressed air. Paige, standing off to one side during the agitation, thought about how neatly Marik had taken the blame off Kaplan's shoulders and wondered why; for say what he might, Marik must know, deep inside, what everyone else could see so plainly: The young man was a prize jack and had made it publicly manifest even before he had tried to provoke a killing. He seemed like a thoroughly unsavory little stinker, and Paige wondered why Marik would even bother.

Marik started to talk again, and they quieted down in a hurry. Ragusa had his unlit cigarette between his lips and kept dropping bits of tobacco on the table, and Ory absently kept brushing them off.

"This valve"—Marik pointed with his stylus at the bright disc at the opening of what they were beginning to think of as Kaplan's tube—"is one of your two crucial points. When the system went down, it jammed open and bled off enough pressure to ground the MAX, here—" He touched the effigy lightly, indicating the stalled MAX farther along the tube where it had swung away in a sharp curve. "It will take a man with good hand tools to drill through the tube and release it manually."

"I'm not sure it can be done that way," Connelly frowned. "We've never run into this problem before. There were always the backups."

"Not this time," Marik reminded them, and Berrey shook his head.

"Mr. Denisovitch, our SO, was rewriting the software for the backup systems when he went under. Diamond's working on them, but—" He spread his hands hopelessly.

73

"The fact that it happened," Marik told them, "made it obvious that your backups were inoperative; and none of the ships have an automatic mechanical system to cover it. Which again is why we need a man down there."

"You need two men," Paige put in unexpectedly. "I've been watching Kaplan's image. He's barely moved since we got here. I'm betting he needs some attention pretty fast."

"You volunteering?"

Paige grinned. "I'll get my kit."

"You said 'two crucial points,'" Berrey reminded Marik, and he resumed his explanation. "The other is here." They craned their necks to see the tube that held Elluvon's MAX. Marik's stylus traced its outline, and they saw that it was slightly off, minutely deformed, describing sort of an oval rather than a smooth cylinder for about twenty feet. "My guess is that the—creatures—outside—"

"The dragons," Berrey assisted. "Captain Riker filled us in."

"The dragons, then," Marik continued, relieved, "have dented the hull and compressed the tube into this off shape."

"No problem," Ragusa grinned. "We'll just blow her on through."

Marik shook his head. "No. At the speed it would be traveling, with all that pressure behind it, the only thing you could blow her through would be the skin of the ship. She'd hit the deformity and broach the hull at the point of impact. Not only would that evacuate the tubes, losing us Kaplan, and send Elluvon out toward Epsilon Bootes, I think, at a respectable velocity, but it would collapse the tube system."

They knew what that meant. The tubes were not mere transportation devices; they were also part of the basic design of the ship and provided a strong interior framework that reinforced the ribbing of the vessel and protected it against the hungry vacuum of space. Broach the tubes and you stood ready to count your personnel losses in high numbers, not the least of whom would be the all-important Elluvon.

"Even after we get Kaplan out," Marik said, "we'll still have to try to back the MAX out." Berrey shook his head, his mouth quirking.

"Gonna be too easy to bilge it," he told him, and Marik replied that they would know more about that when they got in there.

"It's a long way down," Ragusa said thoughtfully, around his limp, unlit cigarette. "It's a long, long way down. You sure you want to go down there?" But there was no one else, and Kaplan and the Elluvon were depending on them, though they did not know it, and because they were the way they were, and each for his own reason, in the end they went.

"Channel open to ComFleet, sir." Miss Jen's voice was apologetic about the long wait, during which Riker had tapped impatiently on his audio pickup from time to time and strode around peering over the shoulders of his bridge personnel as they worked. Now he hit his com stud and indicated the forward screen, which Jen obediently activated. The face that appeared was rather fair, with thinning dark hair and that thick-skinned, very smooth-shaven look some men have, who never quite seem to get the dark shadow off their cheeks. He said his name was McInnes. He looked frightened.

"Paul Riker, Mister McInnes," Riker said quietly. "We have a situation here that—"

"Captain Riker," McInnes interrupted shortly, "this is a stroke of luck. Stand by one." The image switched, and there before them was Vice Admiral Joseph Hastings. There was time for a glimpse only of the flushed face as the old man ran his fingers distractedly through his bushy white hair, apparently talking with some heat to another party; then there was a flicker and a suggestion, there and gone before it could be truly recognized, of open space and a collection, vast beyond measuring, of bobbing blue globes, misty and burning bright, moving as in a titanic slow-motion sea, riding the crests and troughs, moving slowly and steadily forward toward an unknown shore.

McInnes appeared again. "Sorry. Let me try again." This time Hastings was sitting at his desk, hands folded, his hair a little ruffled, like the feathers of a dissatisfied owl. He nodded a few times, as if in answer to a question.

"Riker."

"Admiral, sir." The ship shuddered with a slight impact.

"So you still have the damned thing aboard, eh?"

"No, sir, it was transferred to *Hope* at 09:57 this date. We are experiencing difficulty with our ambient conditions, sir. We seem to have made rendezvous dead center of the migration path of certain insubstantial creatures—"

Hastings started to laugh. "Now, you're not going to tell me about the famous Xholian dragons, are you? How long have you been talking to Donelang Kris?"

"Not long, sir. I tried to suggest we drive them off with armament, but Captain Kris feels that would be an unwise solution."

"Not only unwise, my boy," Hastings chuckled unpleasantly, "but also a helluva waste of ammunition since the dragons, as you call 'em, don't exist!" At Riker's quick protest, he thundered, "I tell you, *they do not exist!*—except here!" He tapped his head with his bunched fingers, so hard it raised an angry little red knot.

"Now, let me tell you something, Riker. You've got trouble enough without going along with the ravings of this—this religious maniac!—who imagines up big nasty space dragons to worship!" A long arm shot out. "Now, we are in communication with the relatives of your Elluvon bug or its government, if any, or its navy, if that's what it is—and it seems that they are a *gestalt*—a group mind —and they want to know, more or less, when and why the Elluvon *you've* got is dying! Maybe you'd like to tell *me!*"

"There's been an accident in *Hope*'s tube system. The Elluvon's MAX is jammed, and the man we sent down to free it is injured and awaiting help. We can't get the Elluvon out until we bail out our man. The pressure would kill him."

"That's too bad," Hastings said heavily. "Fortunes of war."

"I'm afraid I don't understand, sir." He was afraid he did.

"I think you know perfectly well what I'm saying, Riker. This Elluvon is vital to the security of our entire galaxy. There isn't a man in the service who wouldn't willingly give up his life to protect the federation. I'm sure young what's-his-name—"

"Kaplan."

"Young Kaplan would do the same. Be a hero. No question about it." Riker made no immediate comment, and Hastings snapped, "A good officer, Riker, must always be prepared to take the expedient action! You ought to know that by now! You of all people! You're the one, aren't you, who left that Einai Shimshen in the path of a nova for the good of the ship?"

"Yes," Riker said quietly. "Yes, I'm the one. My decision." His hands were shaking, and he took a deep, steadying breath.

"Well, then. That's settled. I'll give you"—he glanced at his chrono—"thirty minutes to get it out of there and into treatment—and report back to me. Any questions?"

"No questions." His voice was remote.

"Good." Hastings gave a short nod, and the screen went blank. Riker sat staring at it for several minutes, while the bridge personnel peered at him surreptitiously from their stations; and the ship rocked every now and then, with the buffeting given it by the dragons.

The trouble with Riker was that he was basically a decent man, and it presented enormous problems in a situation like this, where he was made to weigh the probable good of the galaxy against the certain death of one man. If Riker had been an ordinary fellow, he could have made a command decision and ordered the MAX blown free with no regard to Kaplan's welfare, and that would have been the end of it. But he was afflicted with this decency thing, this sense of moral order, and he could not in all good conscience order Kaplan sacrificed. It had interfered with his military career before, and he thought ruefully that it probably would again if, indeed, he had a career to look forward to. They could hang him from the yardarm for this kind of disobedience, or whatever it was they did nowadays.

It was not that Kaplan was his friend or anything, or even that the ensign was remotely pleasant. He was not. He was a sarcastic, irritating personality whose presence, for a few minutes, was like salt in the soup, a heightening of the sensibilities; after half an hour, he shriveled the mouth and set the teeth on edge. If there was anyone aboard that was the prime choice for a sacrificial victim, and good riddance, it was Kaplan.

But there it was again, you see. The choice was not his

to make. Riker believed, like Mallory's Sir Bors, that he was responsible for his own actions, that he must not be blackmailed into compromising his beliefs, even at the price of the security of the galaxy. It was a ridiculous anachronism, considering the time he lived in, and it seriously hampered his chances for advancement, but it was the way Paul Riker felt about things, and he stuck to it. He was nailed to his truth the same as Christ. There was not anything he could do about it. He had driven the nails in himself. Nor was he sorry about it.

He leaned back in his chair and said to Jen, "ComFleet, please."

The screen flashed to life. McInnes's face and then the face of Vice Admiral Hastings appeared, affable and self-satisfied.

"Well, that was fast. You got it out, eh? What condition was it in?"

"No, sir," Riker said steadily. "It's still trapped. For all I know, it's still dying, or dead. I didn't check."

The smile faded slowly on the face pictured before them, and the expression hardened. "I hope you know what you're doing, Riker."

"Yes, sir. I'm refusing your implied suggestion to sacrifice one of my people to expediency. I want to go on record as making it official."

"All right. All right, then." Hastings leaned forward and folded his hands on his desk, scowling at Riker through his brows. "Let's make everything official, Captain. I order you to remove the Elluvon *immediately* from its entrapment in the tube and to consider expendable any personnel who might inadvertently be lost in the attempt."

"Sir, I respectfully refuse." There was sincere regret in Riker's voice. Recognizing it, Hastings' tone rose in pitch and volume. His face flushed from red to scarlet, and his eyes were wide and angry.

"You what?" he demanded.

"Sir," Riker repeated in the same quiet tone, "I respectfully refuse."

Hastings' scarlet face became purplish with rage and, Riker suspected rightly, from fear. He remembered his own reaction to the terrible armada, the first and only time he had seen it, and he felt a tinge of sympathy for the stalwart old man who, for the first time in his military

78

career, was not in control of the situation. Hastings' red eyes seemed to start from their sockets, and distended veins stood out at his neck and temples. Flecks of spittle foamed at the corners of his mouth, and he was as angry a man as Riker ever hoped to see. When he spoke, it was very soft and very fast, and he almost stuttered in his haste to strike back from his anger and fear.

"Then I charge you, Captain Paul Riker, U.S.S. *Skip-jack,* with one, a violation of galactic security; and two, a violation of Fleet Order #291, regarding the safety of intelligent life forms aboard federation vessels, under Articles 92 and 134, and I intend to convene a general court-martial at the earliest possible date.

"And may I add, Riker," he ground out as an afterthought, "that I will hold you morally and legally responsible for every—last—life!—the Galaxy may lose to those" —His expression wavered for a moment and came apart, and the thick bulldog lips tried to form words and failed —"those blue *things.* You," he said. "Your fault," he said. And then, "I hope you get the death penalty!" Riker watched him with trepidation, not for himself but for the admiral. He looked as if he were about to have a massive stroke. His breath was coming in great asthmatic gasps. He fumbled for a pill and a carafe of water.

"Transfer command!" he ordered, panting, and Riker, holding his eyes through the screen with an unflinching gaze, beckoned MBenga to the command post and relinquished it to him.

On the screen, Hastings swallowed the pill and leaned back painfully, his chest rising and falling quickly. The veins in his neck, above the constricting collar of his tunic, bulged grossly, and on either side of his Adam's apple a pulse throbbed like a drum. His hand reached out blindly, groping for the cutoff stud, distorting hugely as it neared the screen, and hit the switch. The image began to fade, and Riker snapped, "Hold it, Jen!"

"Aye, sir."

The screen froze its ghostly glow, suspended between *Skipjack*'s persistent signal and Hastings' cutoff.

"Contact his medical people and let them know what's happened. Have an emergency unit sent to his office." He tapped the control studs lightly with the edge of his hand, watching the motionless screen, and MBenga gestured Jen to bring up the image. The shadows began to move, became people, became Hastings lying only too still, with McInnes bending over him as he lay back in his chair, and moments later, medics in their controlled, efficient haste turned the screen into a series of close-ups of someone's hand, part of a tunic, seen blurry and shaded, McInnes's left eye, peering past the pickup at something off screen . . .

MBenga signed Jen to cut it off. The screen went to black and went dead, and the sound of Hastings' stertorous breathing filled the bridge for long seconds after the audio went silent.

"Lord God," Riker muttered, staring at the empty screen and speaking to no one in particular, "I hope I haven't killed another one!"

It made them all uneasy, especially MBenga, sitting at the command post, and nobody answered him. Under the buffeting of the powerful flukes outside, the ship rocked constantly, as if under a heavy sea.

Chapter V

Ragusa had been right: It was a long way down, and a long way in, too, through the hollow metal gullet that reflected back the light of the head lamps they both wore and made phosphorescent green discs of Marik's eyes when he looked back occasionally to make sure Paige was close behind him. They were wearing tubesuits, a sort of coverall made of a rough artificial leather, rather like suede, with a high friction coefficient that gave them some stability in the highly polished, sleekly machined curve of the tubes. They appreciated them most especially now, when the ship rocked often and unexpectedly from the dragon blows, and they were flung awkwardly against the sidewalls; the suits prevented inescapable headlong slides down the featureless, frictionless conduits that would have ended inevitably at the bottom of one of the verticals. They were soft-shod in the same fabric. Paige, as he had promised, carried his medical kit. Marik had the necessary tool bag slung at his shoulder and had brought along a sackful of metal cubes he referred to as Johanssen blocks, along with the medical sled for Kaplan. Coiled at his shoulder was a tough nylon rope, attached at one end to a machined rectangle of polished metal almost identical to the blocks except that its attaching face was broader than its depth. On the reverse was a thick staple through the eye of which the rope passed and was secured. Paige, who knew nothing about metallic interfaces, wondered privately whether Marik was not carrying the notion of rescue a bit far. They were going to try to get a spacer out of a transit tube—not a skier off an alpine cliff. Why —there was not even anything to tie Marik's rope *to*. He opened his mouth to say as much, and the ship rolled sharply. The tubes softly *gong*ed, and up ahead of Paige there was the familiar flash of those green discs.

"I'm okay," Paige said into the darkness, and Marik made a sound of assent, stopped abruptly, and went down on his knees cautiously. He bent his head, Paige thought, though it was hard to see. Every so often, the alien officer would kneel and press both palms spasmodically to the bottom of the tubes, and several times Paige thought he heard a faint *hssss, pop!* but he could not be sure. If he had had to guess, he would have thought Marik was praying, for that was the way his mind worked, even though he knew the Einai stood to pray.

After the fourth or fifth—or tenth—episode of this sort, Paige asked Marik if he would mind telling him just what he thought he was doing. The green flash again.

"My job, Doctor," came the amused reply. He got to his feet again, and Paige followed along willy-nilly as he limped carefully, silently, down the endless cylinder.

"I always thought," Paige offered, after a quarter hour's crouched passage, "that the engineers were supposed to know how to fix these things." His voice sounded louder in the silence between the gongs.

"Maybe they did in the olden days," Marik replied after a thoughtful few minutes, "but the maintenance crews probably know as much as the engineers now, about the tubes exclusively, I mean. The engineers have their hands full keeping the piles stable, not to mention computing the mathematics of warp and insuring separation."

"While the computers loaf."

The green discs glinted briefly at him from the tubes ahead. "It's a case of GIGO, my friend," Marik chuckled. "They leave the tubes to the maintenance men—who get

82

hazard pay for it—and the science officers, who don't. We're supposed to know all about them."

"Sounds tough," Paige commented, and Marik made no reply, although he was amused by his choice of words. Tough, eh? Paige—*Duli* Paige—was competent to use the word.

Anyone who had been a jungle *duli* was entitled to the word that best described himself: tough—resilient, strong, robust, stubborn, and very difficult. Well—any of these, alone or in combination, described the jungle doctors of Eisernon. Bush-country doctors, called *dulis* or *tamdulis* after an obscure and compassionate hero of antiquity, tended those peasants who lived on a mere subsistence level in the jungle, fighting off *d'injit* and bandits and ignorance along with disease. Most *dulis* Marik had known were Einai, but occasionally some altruistic Erthlik took up the challenge flung down long ago in the jungles of a little Erthlik country whose name no one remembered.

"We manage," Marik replied tardily, quietly, thinking that the tubes at least were clean, with help nearby if there were problems too involved for one man to handle, and no pathetic peasant mothers bringing you a pitiful little bundle of rags and bones, two days dead, to resuscitate. Marik had spent five years as a *duli* before the war, working under Priyam Oman Shari-Mnenoplan. He knew how they could look at you. It was something you did not soon forget.

"It's a good deal easier than the jungle," he added, and Paige wondered idly how he would know.

A resounding shock, bonging metallically as if they were in an enormous bell, greeted them as they rounded a sharp curve, knocking them both off their feet. The effects of the dragons cavorting was more noticeable here, and the tubes reverberated, tone upon tone, like a mammoth xylophone. Paige grabbed his ears with both hands, smashing his head lamp against the medical sled, remembering the winter he and his brother had rolled down Bartlett's Hill in an old pickle barrel, on a dare. It had been the same feeling, only then it was not a head lamp that got broken but Matt's nose.

Marik had gained his knees, then his feet, and he gave Paige a hand up. It puzzled him that Marik had gained his sea legs so quickly until he reminded himself that the

Einai were cat derived and had an important difference in the structure of the inner ear.

The going became more hazardous, with the effect of walking through a rolling barrel, and each new impact jeopardized their already too insubstantial footing. One savage shock sent Paige bumping ten feet along the side-wall, right past Marik's head, giving him a bad minute or two before the Einai caught him and pulled him back to safety. Paige wished the tubes would stop their infernal measured rolling. It made the going rough, and he was beginning to get a little queasy. Marik, who had been touching each overhead light since the curve, moved more slowly now. The tubes rang sporadically in their ears, and Marik had to raise his voice to be heard. "We're getting close."

"You sure?" To Paige this bit of tube looked like every other. He was glad Marik was along. He would not have begun to know how to get out of here. "How do you know?"

"The overhead lights. They're set every five feet. Compute mathematically and—"

"Oh." He adjusted his medikit. "Oh, all that measuring you did, down in Engineering—"

"Watch your step!" The tension in Marik's sudden command froze Paige where he stood, imaginary hackles rising in prickles down his spine. Marik moved aside slightly and pointed, and there, yawning at his feet, was a sight his mind at first refused to grasp. The frank glare of light shed by Marik's head lamp divulged a gaping channel that arched away into darkness. Hard on the heels of *Thank God I didn't fall into that* came *No wonder Marik insisted on walking ahead of me*. The gullet looked big enough to swallow a fair-sized elephant, although his common sense told him it could not be more than a meter and a half in diameter. *Big enough, thanks.* A crescent-shaped section of thick plating was half retracted into an almost invisible groove in the graceful bend of the tube. Paige repressed a shudder as he recalled how many times within the past half hour he had stepped boldly on great circles inscribed in the metal underfoot, never stopping to think of them as a couple of centimeters of steel over—he leaned forward and Marik's lamp obligingly lit up a sheer drop of some twenty-five to thirty feet—empty space, except that at the bottom of this particular shaft lay Ensign Parry Kaplan, very, very still.

Paige looked up at Marik, who was standing as straight as he could under the low overhead, carefully uncoiling the rope from his shoulder. "He's not moving," he told him. "He could be dead."

Marik shook his head and continued his maddeningly slow unwinding of the rope. "I can see him breathing." *Those damned slit pupils,* Paige thought.

"All the way here, you had to stop and pray every two minutes," he accused mildly. "All right. I don't have anything against praying! But now we're here, and you stand there doing nothing!"

"Praying?" Marik looked puzzled for a minute and then grinned briefly. "Come over here, Doctor." He retraced his steps for a good twenty feet back up the corridor and went down to his knees. Paige crept up beside him, and Marik indicated a red rectangle of what seemed to be transparent metal, but probably was not, fitted seamlessly into the floor of the tube. Marik lay his hands one atop the other and put all his weight behind them as he shoved suddenly against the plate. There was no change. No lights, bells, hidden hatches, or ducts coming down to give you the secret word, which in Paige's estimation, was *out.*

"So?" He was unimpressed. "Nothing happened."

"And something should have," Marik nodded, bracing himself against the sidewall as the ship—and the tubes—rolled slowly again. "Whenever sufficient pressure—air pressure, manual pressure, it doesn't matter—is brought to bear against those plates, the red light goes off, and they snap the valve—over there." He pointed to the crescent-shaped lid half over Kaplan's pit. "This time it didn't. Now we know why he fell, where he is, and what has to be done about it."

Marik moved quickly about his preparations and made Paige feel slow and clumsy by contrast. First he marked the valve with luminous spray and changed the bulb in Paige's head lamp, making the darkness twice as bright. In the glow of both lamps, Paige, too, could see Kaplan crumpled at the base of the drop and the shallow rise and fall of his shoulders. He was curled in a fetal position, his left shoulder upward and his right leg twisted under him at an odd angle. His head was bent so they could not see his face, only the ruffled fair hair that made him look like a small boy.

Marik was still busy with his rope; he uncoiled the last of it and lay it beside him, divesting himself of all unnecessary tools, which he stored carefully in the leather pouch he had carried over his shoulder. Then he took a portable hand drill—Paige wondered why he had not brought a laser gun, which was quick and clean, but Marik shook his head quickly, intent on his work, and said that it could warp the tube—with a fine bit and drilled three neat holes about one and one-half centimeters apart in each direction, describing a perfect triangle, and dropped a cotter pin in each.

"That ought to hold it," he murmured, putting away the drill.

"I'll bite," Paige offered. "Hold what?" And Marik explained that the cotter pins, being made of almost impervious duralloy, would hold the valve open even if the system should go up again, by some remote possibility. Without the pins, the valve would automatically snap shut, and Paige, Marik, and their patient would be caught in the vertical tube without recourse to help. As soon as he had gotten Paige down there to treat Kaplan, he added, he could set about repairing the jammed valve permanently.

"As soon as *who* goes down there?" Paige asked pleasantly, filling a hypo, which he stored in its packet.

"Both of us. You stay, I don't. You're needed there, I here." He began recoiling the rope in a different configuration, and again Paige had the impulse to ask him what, for Pete's sake, he expected to tie it *to* when Marik gave a sheepish smile and offered, "You know, when I was a youngster in training, aboard one of *our* ships"—he clapped the rectangle absently to the sheer wall face, where, its precision-machining having been ground so fine, it stuck fast, clinging like a leech to the mirrorlike surface—"they took us out to demonstrate one of these. It's called a De Belfin device, and I was the only lad who asked what they were going to tie it *to*." He looked a bit shamefaced in retrospect, and Paige swallowed hard, squinted at him, and wagged his head in amazement that anyone could ever have been so ignorant.

"You're *kidding*," he said.

Captain Donelang Kris was sitting quietly on the bridge, contemplating the stars through the great forward ports, when the call came from ComFleet. He lifted a hand, and the ports polarized, the screen flipped down and brightened, and the image of Commander McInnes appeared on the screen of the *Hope,* as it had on *Skipjack.* The blue officer inclined his head gravely.

"Commodore. A pleasure, sir." McInnes seemed upset, and Kris had no wish to aggravate his condition.

"Captain Kris, I'll be brief. We've got a fluid situation here, and it centers around that Elluvon bug. There's an alien armada out there taking up half a sector—it's unbelievable how vast it is!—and the only message we can clear from it is, 'Has the Elluvon died yet?' Now we know that it's trapped in your tube system, but for the sake of the galaxy, you have to get it out!—*any—way—you—can!* We have to keep it alive and get it well—or God knows what that armada will pull. Its retaliatory powers . . . well, you get the picture."

Kris inclined his head again. "We have sent two additional men into the tubes to retrieve your personage 'Elluvon,' " he explained in not terribly good Erthenglish. "One of our physicians and the science officer, Marik, of U.S.S. *Skipjack.* They should emerge shortly."

"They'd better," McInnes warned. "Consider it an order, Captain: I want that bug out of there within the hour— live and breathing—or I'll break every man jack of you down to the lowest spacer aboard!—and ship you to the rim!"

"I understand completely, sir. And most pleasant good wishes to you, also." He rang off and motioned the screen away, and his efficient staff returned to bridge to its previous state. The light of the stars was clear and steady, and Kris mentally chanted three benisons before he shut his eyes and said, "Get me Engineering."

Berrey was alone with Connelly at the grid, watching Marik and Paige's slow progress through the tubes. Ragusa, Ory, and Greco had gone to make the standard hourly check of the piles, and Collins was busy helping Diamond test the software that, this time for certain, was supposed to bring the system up. The wall com chimed, and Connelly got it. He nodded at Berrey.

"Engineering. Berrey."

"Captain Kris here," said the precise metal voice. "Any word?"

"No, sir. We've got a grid fix on them, but it's doubtful how long we'll be able to hold it. Some way those dragons are bleeding off power. If we don't get out of here pretty soon, sir, we'll have to break out the oars, so to speak." It was an old navy saw, and Kris did not dignify it with a comment.

"We will hold," he said instead, "until Priyam Marik and Doctor Paige get their patient clear. Then you are to take any and every available action to extricate the Elluvon being. Understood?"

"Aye, sir. We'll stand—"

A momentous impact, shuddering the whole of the gigantic ship, slammed it broadside and flung small objects shattering to the deck, threw personnel about like puppets, and noticeably dimmed the lights. Berrey got to his feet and ran for the grid, where several red pinpoints indicated breaches in the tubes. He got a glimpse of Paige sprawled motionless on the deck and Marik, writhing as if in pain before he went limp, and the grid flickered out. He returned wearily to the com.

"Bridge," he demanded heavily.

The com chimed. "Bridge." It was the captain's voice.

"Berrey here. We have several breaches in the tubes. Nothing too serious. But the grid collapsed—we're blind as a bat. Not," he added, "that it matters anymore."

"The men?"

Berrey's mouth quirked. "Both of them were down, the last I saw. One of them, Marik, I think, was sort of squirming. They must've lost their air, and—"

"Implement your orders, Mister Berrey," said the captain. The voice was cool and unruffled, and he might have been passing the time of day. For an instant, Berrey hated him.

"Aye, sir." He turned to see Diamond standing there beside Connelly. The big, blond man with the tired, red-rimmed eyes smiled.

"System's up," he said, and Berrey nodded with ineffable weariness.

"Blow the Elluvon free," he said.

It was easier to rappel down a tube than down a cliff face, Paige thought, remembering his survival training, because if your legs got tired you could always stiffen them and suspend yourself with your feet against one wall face and your back against the other. Paige had no trouble along that line, in the thirty-some feet of descent, but he noticed that Marik had to stop and rest twice on the way down. It occurred to him that the duel with Mennon had probably taken more of Marik's reserves than he cared to admit.

It came as a surprise to both of them that the tube Kaplan occupied was a blind shunt that led nowhere; but the major surprise was Kaplan himself.

Paige touched down next to the ensign's inert body and gingerly felt the skull and the back of the neck for palpable damage. Finding none, he switched off his head lamp, carefully lifted his head, and drew back an eyelid, checking the pupil with his penlight for signs of brain damage. Before he could read the result, Kaplan grunted, jerked his head away, and shook it, muttering crossly, "Hey, what's going on?" He rubbed his watering eyes with both hands. "Guy can't even *sleep?*" There was no hesitancy, no tremor in his actions, *probably no upper vertebral injury, anyway,* Paige told himself with relief. He lowered the penlight and switched on his lamp.

"I'm Doctor Paige. How d'you feel?"

Kaplan muttered, "My ankle hurts like hell." He kept squinting reflexively away from the light. Normal pupil response, Paige noted.

"Anything else? Any nausea, dizziness, trouble with your vision?"

"Yeah, some clown keeps shining lights in my eyes."

"Headache, backache, weakness in your arms or legs?"

"No. No, no, no. Just my ankle, and a few bruises." He scowled at Paige, then at Marik, who was just touching down and whom he saw merely as a shadowy man shape with a faceless light for a head.

"Took you guys long enough. Did you get the bug out yet?"

"No," Paige said shortly. "Let me have a look at that ankle." He drew the affected leg out from under Kaplan and got the tight boot off without much help, for Kaplan had his face screwed up tightly and turned away from

89

them. He felt of it with experience born of long practice and gestured at Marik.

"Would you believe this? Not a bone broken, as far as I can tell. Just a very bad sprain. Take a look."

Marik came back from his close inspection of the terminal air jets at the blind end of the tube and, squatting next to them, took the sensitive, swollen ankle in gentle hands and probed it. He slid a glance at Paige.

"Dislocation," he said quietly. "Here—" He placed Paige's hand on the deformity, and Paige shot him an admiring glance.

"Well, I'll be damned! You're right. How did you—"

What Marik did next was quick and professional and as merciful as he could make it. With a firm, even traction, he reduced the dislocation before Kaplan could even yell. Paige immediately began to splint the injury as a preventive measure until they could get the radiology done on it and in case of fracture that might have been overlooked because of the swelling, which was considerable.

"Your patient's a lucky young man," Marik observed, measuring the distance of the fall with his eyes, preparatory to climbing back to the surface. He did not relish the idea of the climb. At the sound of his voice, Kaplan's head flashed up. He looked surprised and disappointed.

"Oh. So it's you," he grunted, holding his thigh just above the knee with both hands, as if he could constrict the amount of pain that would get through to his brain. Marik made no comment to that, but felt of the splints; they were solid and would hold fast during the trip back through the tubes.

"I was hoping he would kill you," he persisted meanly.

"So was he," Marik replied absently, testing the rope for his return climb. "I seem to have disappointed you both." He looked down at Paige, who had finished splinting the ankle and was cleaning up and putting away. "Let's get him out of here. Want to hand me that sled?" They were securing the straps of the emergency sled when Kaplan growled something under his breath. Marik did not look up.

"Say again?" He pulled the chest strap tight.

"I said, I'm not sure I want to be rescued by your kind, Marik. I don't need your charity!" Marik straight-

90

ened and regarded him with cool patience, leaning both hands on the edge of the sled.

"Let's define our situation, Mister Kaplan," he said conversationally. "My purpose in coming down here had nothing to do with an altruistic desire to spare your particular life. Your particular life—or the loss of it!—means nothing to me. But before I can get the Elluvon—who *is* important!—out of here, I have to remove your carcass first. You are, to put it bluntly, impedimenta. You are in the way. You impede progress. I would have had to come down here to remove a meteorite or a container of refuse. It's my job. Nothing personal. Clear?"

"Yes, sir," muttered Kaplan in a chastened tone; as an afterthought, he added, "Ow!" as Paige put the last touch on his leg straps.

"I don't want to bring him up until I've repaired the valve," Marik told Paige. "Too great a margin for error with it jammed like that. Never know when it'll spring loose." Paige nodded once, imagining the valve, snicking swiftly, like some modern guillotine, across a luckless modern neck.

"We'll wait," he said. "Take your time."

Marik climbed painfully up the rope, stopping twice to rest on the way up. By the time he reached the valve, his face was beaded with sweat. He used the half-open valve as a handhold to lever himself out of the tube. He had not really lied to Paige; the possibility existed that the valve would snap shut of its own volition, although that was highly unlikely. More probable was the grimmer consideration that as tough as the *Hope*'s skin was, no hull could hope to withstand those intermittent sledgehammer blows indefinitely. Sooner or later, those insubstantial dragons were going to penetrate the hull and take out a lot of good people, not the least of whom would be Paige, Kaplan, and Marik, not to mention the Elluvon, too, MAX notwithstanding.

He got his tools together and pulled the cotter pins out of the holes he had drilled. He had a little flexible saw, kind of a heavy wire covered with diamond dust, and he threaded it expertly through two holes at a time and proceeded to saw out an accurate triangle of metal plating about a centimeter and half to a side. He hoped he had been accurate in his estimation of where the relay would be and was gratified to find that he had been only a few millimeters off of dead center. The open-shut relay lay right on top, behind and slightly below the level of the remainder of the valve. Marik touched the valve experimentally with his fingertip, lifting it slightly, and it jumped out of his hand and snicked shut, like a trap closing, cutting off Paige's "Hey!" in midsound. Marik realized what had happened. When Kles depressed all the command switches, the valve got hung precariously between obeying two orders: the order to remain open and the systems order to shut. It had been so delicately balanced that the pressure of his fingertip tripped it. He wondered why it had supported his weight when he climbed out on it and decided that the plating he had sawed out had something to do with it. He turned it over and saw the circular depression, quite small, graven into the reverse. He recognized it as a stop, the combination of the retractable peg in the valve and the deeply carved notch in the plating. It was much simpler and more efficient than the key system *Skipjack* used—unless your computer went down, whereupon you were out of luck. Marik reached in and with infinite care touched the switch with an insulated screwdriver; the valve slid open smoothly, then closed again as he flipped the switch, and again, it opened. Unless the system went up again, and there was traffic as usual, they could expect the valve to stay safely open. Marik reattached the missing plate with a special epoxy used for tubes maintenance and filled the three bit holes with globs of it. Puttylike, it was too thick to run but malleable enough to work in varied situations. He polished the end result with emery cloth and then with a special coated metal block that was curved to fit the shape of the tubes. When he was finished, he closed his eyes and ran his fingers across the repaired area. There was no roughness, no discernible periphery between the area he had repaired and the untouched metal. Under the light of his head lamp, there was only a lighter series of lines and dots to mark the place he had mended. He consulted his ticket. The whole repair job had taken slightly over ten minutes. Ten minutes to correct a flaw that had stranded what must be, at this moment, the most important being in the galaxy. He suppressed a tinge of concern over the Elluvon's welfare and leaned over the opening. First things first.

"I've got it fixed. Look, make that rope fast to the end of the sled and you come on up. We can rig the De Belfin as a pulley if we have to."

As it turned out, they had to. Paige came scrambling up the rope seconds after he had attached the rope, surprisingly agile. Marik made the mistake of being audibly grateful to Paige's ancestor apes for his rope-climbing abilities, and Paige gave him a hot answer, and Marik did not understand why; they tried hauling Kaplan up hand over hand, but the rope slipped, and they had to use the De Belfin device, anyway. After that it was easy. Kaplan lay moaning in the main tube, complaining about the fluid pressure in his ankle, from all the lifting and motion, but they had gotten him out, which was why they came here in the first place. Marik gathered his tools into the canvas bag, which he slung over his shoulder, and was reaching up to tap the De Belfin device down, rope and all, with a small hammer when the mammoth shock hit them. If it had been difficult on the power deck, it was insupportably bad here in the tubes. It rattled both men around like peas in a dry shell, like seeds in a gourd. Paige hit the sidewall with a sickening smack and slid down it unconscious to the deck, while Marik, who had smashed his knees and shins on the emergency sled, crumpled to the deck and twisted silently in agony for the moment it took him to slip into a queasy semiconsciousness.

It is interesting to note that Kaplan, strapped firmly into the emergency sled, suffered no damage at all. Because of its conformity to the shape of the tubes, the sled followed the line of least resistance, as it was designed to do, and slid up one wall and around and down another several times, like a carnival ride, and came to rest a few feet away from the two unconscious medics. It was he who first heard the whistles, the thin, high-pitched keening that spelled death to spacemen; but although he tried weakly, he could not call out, for his mouth was completely dry from the healthy jolt of Demerol Paige had given him and from fear; after a while he lay back with his eyes closed, unable to call out, vaguely listening to the air whistle away.

For some reason, the gryphons must have turned on him, for he could feel himself falling endlessly down the

93

sky, turning slowly and lazily in the soft, warm, wet air where it was hard to breathe, where he was smothering for breath; he heard their shrill cries far off somewhere and felt the gashes where their claws had raked his chest and back and the cold, hollow, empty ache of bruised and broken bone. It was the kind of pain that caught his breath up short, and Marik opened his eyes to the dark, still, humid air of the tubes, and a variety of images flooded his consciousness. First, that it was not the rocks below his father's eyries he was lying on but the tool bag with its metal instruments and unyielding Johanssen blocks; and second, that something was wrong with the air, and he found it hard to breathe, and lastly that whistling— The universe clicked together with an audible snap, and he rolled to his knees with an involuntary outcry. Several of his ribs were wet and sensitive to the touch, and his legs were a silent shriek and felt as if they had been soaked in menthol. His knees refused to articulate properly and kept buckling under him, but he crawled across the few yards to where Paige's head lamp marked his position and shook him until he roused.

"Tom! Tommy! Oh, T'ath, here, that's the man, wake up, that's it, come on . . ." Paige sat up suddenly, as if he had had a code three emergency in the middle of the night. He stared blankly at Marik and then rubbed his forehead with a sudden hand.

"What?" he asked thickly. "Are we finished with that one?"

"*Tom!*" Marik was insistent. "Tom, wake up, listen to me! We're losing air! Do you understand? The hull's been broached, and we're losing our air! We've got to get Kaplan back down the tube!"

Paige touched a spot on the back of his head and winced. His eyes focused on Marik. "You're hurt," he said slowly, and Marik shook his head impatiently.

"Try to listen, Tom. When you get back to the tube, take this spanner"—he handed Paige a tool—"and twist the air jets to the right, do you understand. *To the right.* Not far, a quarter turn should do it. That'll give you fresh air until we can get you out of there."

Paige took the tool in limp fingers, looking confused. His breathing was a series of shallow gasps, and his lips, in the bad light, looked distinctly blue. "What about you?"

he asked as Marik propped himself up against the wall, ignoring the explosions of fireworks behind his eyelids as he bore weight on the legs and retrieved the sled with Kaplan on it. The rope was still connected to the De Belfin device, which had kept the sled from slipping into the open shunt, and Marik helped Paige lower Kaplan and himself back down the tube they had tried so diligently to escape. The trap had become a refuge, and they welcomed it. Just before he slipped down the rope, Paige realized that Marik had no intention of joining them, and he asked, suddenly, "But—what about you?" and Marik forced a travesty of a smile and told the smothering Erthlik that he would be down shortly, that he was not to fret about it, and please to remember the air jets, a quarter turn to the right. He made his way to the pressure plate down the tube and managed—he could not have said how —to get down and throw his weight upon it, closing the valve. He heaved a sigh of relief. At least Paige and Kaplan were safe. He leaned back against the curved side-wall for the space of two breaths, willing the pain to a bearable level, trying to force it back down from his consciousness. People thought that if you were a telepath, you were some kind of a superman, a demigod, who could exercise some kind of superb control under any and all conditions. Well, maybe you could, sometimes; but times like this, when you were hurt and could not breathe very well even if you *were* used to the rarefied atmosphere of gryphon flight, being a telepath did you about as much good as an Olympic swimmer's talent would do him under the same conditions. Only, you could push the pain away. A little. Enough to plan. The air was getting thinner, and it had to be stopped. Somebody had to plug those holes. You, Marik. He hoped Paige had remembered the roses. No. The air jets. Had to have air. Could not live without air. He felt for his broken ribs with a cautious, fumbling hand and encountered the tool bag instead. The tool bag. Tools in it, and the blocks. The Johanssen blocks. Blocks, rocks. He shook his drooping head in annoyance at the thought that kept buzzing around in it, whining like a mosquito, like air escaping from a ship. He wanted to sleep. Air escaping.

Air.

Escaping air.

His hand closed on the block, and he had his answer. He levered himself up from the deck with a monumental effort, trying to think clearly, keeping his thoughts concentrated on one idea alone: Block the air from escaping. Find the places where the hull was pierced and close them. His back and knees were bleeding badly, and blood pounded in his temples and ears. He had to keep popping his ears to ease the sharp ache that kept building up with the loss of pressure.

He found the first perforation because he was an alien, because his sharp Einai ears could hear the source of the all-pervading whistle more easily than could an Erthlik's ears; the rest he found because he was clumsy and weak and tired.

He could not see the little hole he plugged with the smallest metal block because it was tiny and there was no contrast between the darkness of space outside and the darkness of the tubes. Marik wondered, with a small part of his mind, where his head lamp could have gone, but it did not matter. What mattered was that now there was one less squeaky, steady whistle measuring the moments left to him. He let his hand slip wearily down the sidewall below the block, and suddenly it was caught up short with a stabbing cold pain at the palm; he realized that he had found yet another fault. He pressed his hand to the spot and fumbled another block out of the bag and replaced his hand with a smoothly worked Johanssen block. Good old Johanssen block, he thought foggily. Good old Johanssen. Somebody ought to give him a medal. He started patting the sidewall with both hands, like a drunk trying to find a keyhole, and found instead half a dozen more perforations that he methodically blocked. He worked well, like an automaton, oblivious of the pain now and the sticky wetness in his boots and unconcerned about the persistent white blotches that kept coming up into his vision from some nether region and exploding silently just where he happened to be focusing at the time. What bothered him was the roses, the smell of sun-warmed roses that Mishli had planted on the south side of the pavilion. There should not be roses here, but then, Mishli should not be here, either, and twice he thought he had seen her standing just out of sight, just off the edge of his vision.

The whistles had stopped now, and the ship was rocking

as if she were at anchor on a gentle swell, just off the pier below the pavilion, where the cormorants and the *standi* perched on the mossy rocks to dry their wings. Marik felt very tired and wanted to sit down, but he heard a soft *hsss, pop!* of a valve opening, and there was a breath, a current, cool and heady, coming from Kaplan's tube. Marik took a deep breath, then another and another, and felt his head begin to clear. His ears popped again, and the insane tickles stopped running down his back at last, and his soggy waistband began to get cold. Marik took a few more deep breaths and found himself shivering uncontrollably. But there was air! Blessed air! Clean, cool, and sweet, it blew away the hot, humid stillness and Mishli, and her roses.

Marik made his way to the edge of the shunt and lay against the cool metal, drinking the air like a toper, in great gulps and draughts. The metal was cool against his cheek and unbelievably smooth, and he was content for the moment just to lay there, accepting his need for rest with the instinct of a wounded animal, shivering with shock and weariness. Light was streaming out of the opening with the heady, oxygen-rich air, blossoming out as if it were a tree of light, its roots in the opening. Shadows moved down below, changing the configuration of the light, shifting the patterns the way a wind would strum the branches. There was the sound of voices.

"Hey!" Paige called. "Hey—Marik! Are you all right up there?" Marik took a breath to answer and let it out again, smiling against the metal. He should have known they wouldn't let him rest. He hauled himself to his elbows and peered over the slope.

"Here," he said. Paige peered at him critically and dug into his medikit for a plastex vial, which he tossed up to him. "Here," he said, "take two of those A.S.A.s and one of the other—the scored tablet." The one glimpse he had had of Marik's face frightened him. The Einai's skin was fish-belly pale, almost as light as a fair earthling, and even from where he stood, Paige could see the telltale shuddering of physiological shock. Marik swallowed the pills and threw the vial back to him, resting his head on his folded arms. Paige picked up the loose end of the rope, coiling it preparatory to throwing it up to Marik, when suddenly, high above, the overhead lights went on. There was a deep-throated vibration beginning somewhere in the bowels of the ship, the feeling of immense power held in check, and frankly canned, recycled air began to eddy around them, exclusive of the narrow jet stream that came from the nozzles Paige had turned. Marik was nowhere to be seen.

"Marik!" he called. "What's going on?" And the Einai, who had gotten to his feet with a semblance of his usual alacrity, put his face over the edge of the shunt to report that the system was up.

"We're getting out of here," he exulted. "After all this —we're going to get him out of here, after all. You know," he confided quickly, so quickly that his words tended to run over each other in their haste, "I couldn't understand at first why the valve should open and give out the fresh air just when I needed it. It was supposed to stay closed, you know, until the MAX—or whatever—depressed the terminal stud in Emergency. It was like a miracle!" He moistened his lips with a dry tongue. "And then I figured that this system must be rigged so that unless the following pressure plate is depressed in sequence, you see, the valve just automatically springs open again. So I don't suppose it was a miracle, after all." His eyes clouded, remembering roses. "Though it seemed like one, for a while there," he added quietly.

"Who can say?" Paige shrugged. "You're here to tell about it, aren't you?" He hoped he had not given Marik too large a dose of the Methedrine. He had been so intent on treating for shock that he totally forgot about the Einai metabolism: fast, sensitive, hyper— He hoped he had not done more harm than good. Marik's head came up with a flash, and Paige craned his neck. "What's the matter?" he called.

Marik looked down at him with the old aloof intensity, like a big cat on the hunt, every nerve alert, every muscle tense. "I'm not sure," he whispered. "Something metallic— and big!—on the edge of my mind . . ."

He could not place it, could feel its approach, its mindless brute bulk, but he could not pinpoint the danger until his eye fell on the pressure plate far down the tubes, almost at the bend. As he watched, the glow in the glassite rectangle changed from warning red to go-ahead green. The realization of what that meant chilled his bones.

"Oh, great Tadae," he muttered to himself. "Something's gone wrong! They're sending another MAX through!"

Behind him, he heard the distinctive *hsss, pop!* of the valve cutting off his last avenue of escape.

Chapter VI

It was surprising how calm he felt, Dao Marik thought, how much in control of his remaining resources he found himself, compared to his sorry state of only a short while ago. True, the pain of his injuries still lanced him dully when he moved wrong, but Paige's medication had pushed it off somewhere and was holding it, along with his mortal weariness, at bay. For the duration of the drugs, at least, he was integrated with himself again and glad of it. He was going to need it.

He was trapped in the tubes, and they were sending a MAX through, and there was no way out. That much was absolute. But he did not intend to die yet, either, and his feeling about that was just about as absolute as a finite being could get. He made a quick mental inventory of his assets: the tool bag on his shoulder; the De Belfin device still clinging to the wall; the jutting Johanssen blocks covering the perforations in the ship's skin; there was not much else in the featureless mirror curve of the tubes but Marik himself. My best asset, he thought wryly. It would have to be enough. He had no wish to become the first two-dimensional Priyam in the history of ComFleet. He began to trot painfully down the tubes, away from the direction of the danger. He had left the blocks where they were. Pulling them free would only have increased the size of the perforations in the weakened metal; but he had taken the De Belfin along. He could not have said why.

The air was thinner, and his head was getting light. Somewhere there was the muted rhythm of the pumps. His ears popped.

It would not be the MAX that would get him, he thought, not the friendly robot MAX, with its limited, cheerful, metallic vocabulary; it would be the tube case, the big, mindless hulk that fit the tubes with only a centimeter to spare all the way around. Not the MAX; the tube case.

The tube case that held the MAX was streamlined, whereas the MAX was specialized; it facilitated the MAX's safe passage through the tubes, where the MAX's many rims, handles, paks, and protuberances would have been irrevocably damaged. The tube case's only claim to special devices was a narrow, rubber-edged bumper, some eight centimeters wide, that ran around the case's slightly bulging leading end and was used as a stop in holding shunts, where air pressure might not have had time enough to build up a cushion.

His ears popped again as the pressure was lowered to pull the MAX through at its breakneck pace. It was going down fast; they are putting it through on a *RedBlanket* code, he thought, and his nose suddenly spouted blood. His ears sang. There was a whisper, a presence, and there came the MAX in its tube case, big, heavy, and fast. Marik tried to run then, to escape the juggernaut bearing down on him, but his legs gave out and he sprawled in the tubes, the contents of his tool bag scattering widely. He sucked air through his clenched teeth, partly because of the pain and partly because he expected the tube case to run him down, but instead, there was a series of sharp reports that echoed down the tubes and away, and the Johanssen blocks that had covered the perforations came whistling past him, one of them barely grazing his cheek. The hollow whistling began again, in a much lower note—the metal tore, Marik thought wildly, and the perforations opened up—and even as Marik scrambled to his feet, grabbing whatever tools he could find, he saw that the case had slowed perceptibly and was just now beginning to pick up speed again. He made the only move he could: Slinging his tools out of the way, he watched his chance and leaped for the face of the tube case and caught the rubber stop in a death grip. He hit the convexity with a sharp smack that threatened to drop him off into the path of the case, but he clung desperately to the bumper and quickly drew his legs into the circle, balancing precariously, for the stop was narrow, and the convexity made his position dangerously temporary. The tube case bumped raggedly a few times more, threatening his position even further, and he could see the silver flash of the Johanssen blocks he had spilled shooting away down the corridor. At least it can't happen too often, he thought, since only two of the cube's surfaces had been machined to the almost imperceptible curve required for tube work; if any other surface hit the curve, it would simply fail to adhere. The blocks had but one virtue: They bought him time.

Now that the immediate problem of being run down by the tube case was temporarily solved, Marik had time to consider the second, and more dangerous, situation: the case he was riding had been sent through at its top speed, with pressure pumped in behind it and bled off ahead to increase its velocity until the three-quarter mark was reached. At that time, pressure would be allowed to build up in front of his tube case, to provide a cushion of compressed air to literally blow the Elluvon's MAX clear of its entrapment. But Marik had argued, and he still believed —knew!—that if that much pressure was brought to bear on the second MAX, it would not spring free and speed toward Emergency, as the engineers hoped it would; instead, it would burst the skin of the ship and blow the entire tubes system, not to mention itself, to kingdom come.

He had to prevent that from happening. He had to slow his own MAX down. He had to pull—not blow—Elluvon free while it was still alive. His legs were cramping. He shifted minutely, and his hand brushed a metal knob. Hex nuts. There was a ring of hexagonal nuts attaching—memory flooded back and with it, relief—the safety hatch to the front of the tube case. The safety hatch. *Skipjack* had no such refinements in her small-bore sled tubes, but *Arnumatek* had. All the big systems had safety hatches on

102

their tube cases. There was a certain tool— He groped cautiously through his tool bag, the floor of the tubes skimming by so close he could have reached out and touched it. His fingers read messages back to him: hammer, epoxy, Johanssen blocks, riveted together by their surfaces. He considered placing them against the tube case as a sort of handle to increase his stability (which at present was dependent on the case's velocity, eight centimeters of rubber stop, and the ever-increasing air pressure in the tubes), but realized that the flat blocks would never adhere to the convex surface of the tube case, and the curved face would be even less satisfactory. His fingers hit the drill —and stopped. There was an attachment, a wrench—he fumbled for it and remembered the sight of it spinning ahead of the tube case, down the conduit. Call it fifteen minutes before he collided with the MAX.

Very well, then. He would have to do without a wrench. He took the drill with its carbide bit and went at the center of the nut, but the bit could not get a purchase and kept slipping off, scoring the soft metal of the hex nut, and he snatched a hammer and whanged away at it a few times, nearly knocking himself off the bumper. He tried again, applying the high-speed drill to the flattened metal, and carefully drilled out the center of the nut, through the squashed dome of it and through the bolt it secured. Thank T'ath it is soft metal, he thought. If they had been big, heavy things, or made of one of the exotic alloys that were on the market now, he would never have gotten through them. He wondered who he should thank for cheap materials.

A sudden easing of resistance told him he was through. He moved to the next one. The hammer was unbelievably heavy in his hands, and even the powerful hand drill, with its specially augmented torque, seemed heavy and slow-moving. The pressure was building up in the air around him. The mirror surface of the tubes whisked by inexorably. Somewhere up ahead was another MAX.

Through. Six more to go.

Inside it was the Elluvon. He wondered if it was still alive. The case hit a Johanssen block like an explosion and jolted, nearly throwing him off. He dropped the drill, and the whirling bit ripped through his tube suit and chewed into his thigh, not much, but enough. He swore under his breath, then picked it up and started on the third nut. Even that bought me time, he thought grimly. Even that.

By the time he reached the last nut, his face was running with sweat, and his legs were numb from crouching in the same position. Blinking the sweat out of his eyes, he stuffed the drill back into the tool sack and began to rock the hatch cover he crouched on, shifting his weight back and forth, back and forth, until he felt a corresponding response in the metal. A narrow crack, here and gone, here and gone, appeared at the edge of the hatch. Marik swung harder, the back edge of the cover hitting the sidewall, the motion tugging at him; he broke fingernails, clinging to the slick rubber, as he kept it up.

One more swing, and he used all his force on the backswing; the crack gaped. He thrust his hand into the opening, and the cover swung back, crushing it with the weight of his body behind it, but he clung doggedly to the edge. Wet green lines ran tickling up his sleeve as he let go the bumper with his left hand and clumsily drilled out the last bolt with it, taking at least twice as long as the others had and making a poor job of it.

Done!

The hatch cover slipped out from under him, and he scrambled up its brief, precarious foothold in the instant it took to fall away from him into the tubes and clang and rattle along ahead of the MAX; he pulled himself in, juggling the drill and barking his shins nastily on the edge of the tube case. But he was in! He was in!

He sat crouched and shaking in the scant foot of space between the MAX and its enclosing case, perhaps for five full seconds; then he turned and began to work on the MAX proper. While Marik was not familiar with tube cases, he was an old hand at repairing MAXs, and he had the end plate opened down and the sealant spread over the exposed wiring in seconds. Another moment and he was inside. The exterior pressure was so great that he dared not bring the MAX to earth-normal, but left the end plate open while he worked on the opposite plate and hatch, lying flat on the cool plastex scanslab inside. He could feel the drugs wearing off even as he worked, and the air rushing past was an urgent soporific; but this time he was working on the hatch from the easy side, and it went fast. The hatch leaped free, the end plate went down and flat, and Marik spread the sealant and gathered himself for what he hoped would be the last real physical exertion he would have to sustain before getting home safe.

He closed the panel on the tube case's leading face, feeling his drastically slowed vehicle begin to pick up speed almost immediately, and jumped off the open end plate to the rear, hit, and rolled like a gymnast, coming at last to the curve they had just passed, where he fetched up shakily and got to his feet, watching the MAX go on toward the Elluvon without him. He turned and ran back for Kaplan's tube.

If the air pressure had been great in front of the rushing MAX, the pressure behind it, pushing it along, was titanic. Marik felt as he had once when, as a young lad, he had gone on a ramper hunt off the reef at Bru-Riga and had gone too deep. They had had to dive for him, while he hung motionless there in the blue-green depths, listening to much the same music as there was here. Pretty.

He shook his head. Have to stay clear, he thought, have to keep my thoughts straight. Inhaling was easy. It was exhaling that was difficult. Running did not make it any better. For a moment, he thought he heard the music again. Ridiculous.

The MAX must be right on top of the Elluvon now. He ran faster, or tried to. When he finally heard the sonorous low tones getting nearer, he nearly collapsed with relief. Somewhere here, he thought, pulling out the container of epoxy, somewhere here.

He found the air jets that were spurting out the powerful pressure, three sets of them, imbedded in the curved floor plates, and he stuffed some of them with maintenance epoxy and covered the rest with the fast-drying wiring sealant. It bulged, but it held. He wondered numbly what they would think about *that* down in Engineering, and taking his drill, he limped painfully to the outer wall and began drilling holes in the skin of the ship, deliberately opening the tubes to the vacuum of space.

The commander of the Krail battleship *Mactau* was a man by the name of Win hild-Sar, who had a record of victorious battles from the arenas of the Imperium, where he had defeated even the Imperator's champion, to Minsoner, whose fleet he had personally decimated.

Physically, he was virtually identical to every other member of his race: tall, lean, fine-boned, and extremely blond. Hair, skin, teeth, eyes, were washed to a pastel image of a humanoid, a faded impression, an old memory. One almost expected to see light through their flesh when they passed a window. In the smart black uniforms and jackboots they affected, they appeared ghostly and not quite present, a psychological point in their favor. Their habitual battle silence and insubstantial appearance had the same disconcerting effect on their enemies as the war paint and shrieks of the red Indians of antiquity. That pleased the Krail. It was what they wanted. Terror was part of their battle strategy. That their appearance lent credence to their reputation of being something more—or less—than human was, to their way of thinking, a concomitant of natural selection, a mutation upward. They assisted this trend by relentlessly destroying any baby who failed to come up to the legally required standards. To compensate for the resultant loss in numbers, privileged members of the community, notably the officers of the military and certain government officials, were permitted multiple consorts, to ensure the Imperium of a reasonable number of citizens, all of them of the right sort.

Hild-Sar himself had five consorts—or was it six? It was hard to remember. And at present, he had more important things on his mind than one consort, more or less. At present, hild-Sar was sitting cross-legged on a low table of polished monkey-wood in the splendor of Kles Mennon's personal quarters aboard the pirate ship *Tsai*, waiting for the elusive Einai bandit to deliver the extragalactic Elluvon, as he had contracted to do. But since he had entered, the Einai had said not a word. A Krail aide, clearly a turncoat, had shown hild-Sar to his seat and poured the wine, and there had been an albino swamplander strumming a finger harp from his place in the corner until Mennon's eyes flicked to him and out, and he melted away like snow.

Mennon sat silently opposite him now, each hand hidden in the opposite sleeve of the gold-trimmed scarlet velvet robe that covered his body completely from its high

106

collar to its crenulated hem. On anyone else, hild-Sar thought (himself, for instance, not that he would consider wearing so effete a garment), the robe would have looked impossibly precious; but on this black-bearded green pirate, who wore it with such arrogant ease it was almost contempt, it fit somehow, like a subtle joke on everyone else. Hild-Sar did not understand the mechanics of his reaction, nor did he care to pursue them, although the reaction was the same regarding the single gold hoop in Mennon's ear. It suited him, somehow.

Hild-Sar broke the silence of many minutes with an appreciative sip at his wineglass, which, he noted, was made of intricately cut crystal. "An impudent little vintage," he commented. *He believed that was the proper response to Erthlik wines.* And Mennon, pulling himself back reluctantly from whatever dark thoughts had clouded his tiger-yellow gaze, showed his startlingly white teeth in a smile that did not touch his eyes.

"Pinot Noir, '24, is *not* an 'impudent little vintage,' my dear Commander," he corrected charmingly, sipping from his own glass, "nor is it amusing, modest, or any of the other superior little adjectives one likes to attach to lesser wines. This wine"— he lifted the glass with his bandaged hand—"this lovely wine, is a work of art." He inhaled its bouquet and drank of it, savoring every drop that rolled on his tongue.

"Permit me to hope," the commander offered coolly, "that your wound is not serious."

Mennon turned the hand over carelessly and regarded it with a moment's introspection. "No," he said, from a great mental distance. "No, it's not." He changed the subject abruptly, almost curtly. "You'll want to know about the Elluvon." He took an impatient turn up and down the room, restlessly, and paused, absently toying with the myraid knots of a *bun* tapestry that hung across half the paneled wall.

"I don't have it," he said, and added quickly: "I know where it is, who has it—and how to get it! But I need more firepower."

Hild-Sar stretched out his long legs and regarded the tips of his shiny black boots thoughtfully. "It would be difficult," he mused, "to find myself paying for merchandise that has not been delivered." He pursed his lips and tucked in his chin, watching the pirate with expressionless ice-blue eyes. Mennon smiled again.

"It would be even more difficult, Commander, for you to discover the Elluvon's whereabouts without my assistance."

A gallows smile touched the commander's bloodless lips. "I don't suppose you would be impressed by threats of violence to your person, Master Mennon—even though you have chosen to lie off one of His Imperial Majesty's bravest warships. And one that is best equipped, I might add, for any eventuality." He did not elucidate upon the possibilities, but Mennon had an active imagination.

"Are you threatening me, Commander?" he asked softly, and hild-Sar sipped his wine again and took his time replying.

"Let us say," he ventured, "that I am trying to protect His Imperial Majesty's best interests."

"Then you will understand," Mennon smiled apologetically, "why I felt it necessary to protect my own." He drew back the heavy draperies to reveal half a dozen unpleasant-looking men, armed with *viith* and needlers. They stepped forward and formed a semicircle behind the Krail officer, who shrugged slightly and sighed.

"Shall we say, half now and half when the Elluvon is delivered?"

"Let us say, three-quarters now," Mennon countered reasonably, "and the remainder if you survive. If you do not, I hereby relinquish my claim to the monies owed me." He folded his arms. "I think that's fair—don't you?" The Krail hesitated, and a foot shuffled restlessly behind him. He moved his shoulders uncomfortably.

"I don't have it with me," he muttered. "It'll have to be beamed across." Mennon smiled broadly.

"I'm sure that can be arranged, my dear Commander," he said, and still smiling, ushered him out. "Oh," he added as an afterthought, handing it to him, "don't forget your wine."

Thirty minutes later, Mennon was sitting on the bridge of the *Tsai*, wearing the customary grey uniform of the now-defunct Einai chosen regiment, which had been cut to bits in the initial phases of the Krail/Federation conflict. He wore no color bands or helmet, and there was a nonregulation *viith* slung over his shoulder in a worn

108

leather sleeve. Commander Win hild-Sar was sitting beside him in the seat usually reserved for the first mate, as they prepared to get under way. Mennon slipped off the *viith* and set it at his feet while he strapped in snugly, and for one brief moment, hild-Sar considered snatching it up and holding Mennon prisoner with it. No one would dare harm him while Mennon was at his mercy—would they? And there was a price on his head, flattering by its very generosity. Then the temptation passed, defeated by the logical realization that he would be unlikely to get off the bridge alive once he touched that *viith*. He glanced up and saw Mennon watching him with tiger-bright eyes. "I would advise against it," he said softly, and hild-Sar straightened slowly.

"I trust His Imperial Majesty will not mistake your hospitality to me for something—ah—less complimentary to your intelligence."

"There is nothing," Kles Mennon muttered, sliding a sidelong glance at him, "at all—wrong with my intelligence! My security, now, is a different matter. With your esteemed ship following so close in my wake, as it were, I get the distinct impression of being breathed upon by an ox. I don't particularly care for it." He interrupted himself to make certain adjustments on the panel before him, and played the studs like several measured chords of silent music before he added, "You, my friend, are my insurance against some eager young gunner trying to collect the price on my head—and my head—the moment we sight our target. Not to mention his understandable wish to retrieve the contract money you had sent across." He gave a little mocking bow. "New credits, small denominations—you missed your calling, Commander. You would have made a creditable outlaw."

There was a chill silence, and then hild-Sar lifted his chin.

"You understand," he reminded Mennon stiffly, "that our agreement relegated any and all survivors to our slave pens, to be disposed of as we see fit. I trust you will honor that pact."

"In all but one regard," Mennon answered slowly, his manner growing grim. "You can have them—all!—but one man. His name is Dao Marik. Priyam Hanshilobahr

109

Dom Dao Marik. He belongs to me." His fist clenched. "Alive."

Win hild-Sar thought about it for an instant only and then nodded once. "Done," he said.

It might just work, Dao Marik thought, listening to the air whistle out through the holes he had drilled—fifteen in all, the number of Johanssen blocks he had in his tool bag. It might just work, after all. His nose was bleeding again, and he wiped it against the rough suede of his tube-suit sleeve. He was beginning to get a few mild belly cramps, and he hoped it was not what he thought it was. The fluctuations in pressure had been fairly severe. He put the thought from him and heard the sound he had been hoping for: the whisper of a MAX case, coming toward him from up the tube, and reluctantly, a brief, grating rumble that became a second whispering hum. He fought down the exultation that threatened to overcome him; he *thought*—it *sounded* like—the Elluvon's MAX had pulled free, but it was too early to tell. The next few moments would be the significant ones.

The MAX came barreling down the conduit, end plate open like a hungry mouth, toward Marik and the deliberate perforations in the ship's hull. Theoretically, the air rushing out of the tubes would cut the pressure to the extent of pulling the tube case back toward the holes, and the terrific pressure buildup between the two MAXs would have thinned with the distance, become less and less, until it became a negative pressure and literally sucked the Elluvon's MAX out of its trap. But you couldn't be sure. You were never sure until you could demonstrate the success of your experiment. Or its failure, in which case Marik wouldn't survive to be embarrassed.

The great tube case hurtled toward him, growing larger and more formidable by the second, making his hearts squeeze painfully; and then it suddenly slapped itself against the sidewall with a screeching slam that shook the tubes themselves. Marik, trembling, closed his eyes and opened them again. The tube case had stopped in good time. There was a full three centimeters between the open end of the metal case and Marik's unprotected belly.

It took exactly two and one-half minutes for Marik to plug up the holes he had drilled with the trusty little

Johanssen blocks and another minute and a half to cut a piece of rigid plastex out of the MAX proper to repair the larger rent in the sidewall caused by the tearing off of several closely placed Johanssen blocks. Marik spent another few minutes on his knees with severe cramping and muscle spasm before he could drill through and trip the valve on Kaplan's tube, help Paige haul Kaplan out, and get the valve shut again. At Paige's insistence, he crawled into the open MAX, and Paige shut it up and programmed it for treatment of decompression and shock, but not before Marik caught his sleeve.

"Down the way," he said tightly, teeth clenched against the presence of bubbles in his bloodstream. "About twelve feet back—we must have missed it in the dark. I just saw it—a minute ago."

Paige retraced his steps for the indicated distance and stopped dead. There, faintly traced in the slick curve of the wall, was the outline of an emergency hatch. His jaw dropped, and he shook his head in disbelief. Oh, no, he thought, oh, no, not after all that time down there in the shunt, not after all Marik's gone through, from the look of him. It couldn't be this easy.

He reached across like a man in a dream and pulled the recessed release bar. The hatch popped open and slid up obligingly along an outer wall he could not see. It opened into a bright room with a desk, behind which a middle-aged nurse sat writing something in a book. She looked up with expressive brown eyes, and Paige recognized her as Kraut Annie, the floor nurse for 42 West.

"Why, Doctor Paige," she asked, only mildly surprised, "whatever are you doing in there?" A couple of orderlies started toward him on the run, and Kraut Annie came, too, looking concerned.

"The—the Elluvon," Paige stammered, realizing at last how tired he was. "The Elluvon—and Kaplan. Priyam Marik got 'em out."

Marik, safe and already being treated in his MAX, heard the hatch pop up, saw the light change, and best of all, heard, among the solicitous murmurs, Paige affirm what he had hoped most: Both Kaplan and the Elluvon were safe. Alive—and safe.

Then, and only then, did Dao Marik permit himself the luxury of passing out.

Marik opened his eyes from a restful dream feeling whole and entire. Two hours in a MAX had restored his blood gases to normal, and his wounds, expertly treated, scarcely bothered him. He turned his head, saw Tommy Paige hesitating at the door, and sat up as he came in.

"I thought you were asleep," he ventured, and Marik shook his head and yawned, stretching luxuriously, like a cat, and wincing at his taped ribs in the middle of it.

"Not at all, Doctor," Marik said pleasantly. "Come on in." He pulled on a pair of fatigues that were neatly folded (with his bed's clean linen, clearly intended for the next occupant) on a chair next to his bed. "You're lucky to have caught me. I was just getting ready to leave."

"Yeah, well, I'll make it short," Paige said. "Thanks for taking me down there—I learned a lot—and thanks for getting us all out. I appreciate it. You're a helluva guy." He looked embarrassed and sincere, and he offered his hand, which Marik shook.

"Why do you keep trying to kill yourself?" he accused mildly, and Marik surprised him by what he said next.

"Tom," he asked, half sitting on the edge of the bed, "can you understand the Low Einai chant? I want to tell you a story." Mystified, Paige nodded.

"I think so," he replied, interested. "Yes. I'd like to hear it." And Marik began to chant:

> There is a story told about the sage called Antim-a, who lived long ago in the Time of Wisdom. It happened that there were two villages that had been feuding for many, many generations, so that men could not remember the beginning of their feud. Their villages were small and poor, and they spent their time in war and thoughts of war, in schemes to defeat the other and in building compounds for captives. So that their fields lay fallow, and their animals suffered, and their few children went unwashed and hungry.
>
> Now, Antim-a had been born with a mark upon him, so that he was unable to tell a lie. And for this reason he had no home either in a village or in a city but traveled from one place to another and did not speak until he was asked

to speak; for of all the things that men avoid, it is hearing the truth.

Now it came to pass one day that Antim-a was journeying through the villages, that is, the villages that were poor from their feuding. And they said unto him, Antim-a, master of truth, give us one word to live by. Each village headman had it in his heart that the old man would give some word to tell which was the greater village, or the wiser, or the stronger, and thereby they would be the master of their neighbors, and they would lie under their heel. And the sage said unto them that they would not like his word and would seek him out to kill him; but they swore they would not.

Therefore, Antim-a told them to come in the morning unto the high place, with all the villagers gathered, even to the youngest, and he would give them his word. And they gathered, even to the youngest and suckling babes, to hear what the sage would say. And the sage looked down upon them from his high place and said, "All the people of both your villages are doomed to die, and there is no recourse."

And with this he went away and hid himself, for they sought him out with flails and rods to kill him. But they found him not.

And the people were sore afraid and said, "Let us cease our warring and build up a wall, even surrounding both villages, so that the enemy may not take us by stealth." And they built up their wall and dug wells within the city for water when a siege might come upon them: for they believed all that the old man had said, hearing but not understanding, seeing and yet remaining blind. And they forgot their feud in fear of the unknown enemy.

Many years passed [Marik chanted], and the city had prospered, and Antim-a came that way once more. And the elders of the city, who remembered the prophecy, came out to meet him and said, "Antim-a, you have told a great lie." And he said, "I have not told a lie, neither am I able to lie, or my life would be one of ease and comfort, and I would have a place to lie my head. But I have told the truth."

And they said to him, "See, we have built a wall about our villages, which are become a city, and our wells are deep and clean. And we are a multitude, so that we have made even another city, off to the east, and have prospered. We open our hands to the poor out of our bounty, and they are filled. But you told us that we must die."

"And so you must," said the sage Antim-a; "for who is conceived that does not die? And who is born who lives in his body forever? But in the time between, have you not lived more fully in this form and made your numbers many? So that you have built even another city off to the east, where your sons and daughters thrive? Your caravans are rich, and the princelings pay tribute to you. The poor rejoice; you rule with a merciful hand. Therefore, do not say, 'Why must we die, let us prepare against it, and protect ourselves.' Rather say, 'How must we live, that we may live forever.'"

And Antim-a took up his staff and went away to give truth to another place.

Paige looked up from an introspective study of his hands and said in the ensuing silence, "I see. I see. You really aren't trying to die, after all, then."

"Oh, no," Marik said. "It's the other way. Like it says in the chant. I'm trying to live."

There was more that Paige wanted to say, but the wall com interrupted them to announce that Priyam Marik was wanted down in the morgue, stat, and both of them thought the same thing: the Elluvon.

"Well, well, well," Mykar Sharobi grinned sourly at Marik, straightening up from the alien cadaver he was working on, "aren't you a beautiful sight!" Marik, bruised and bandaged, made no rejoinder to that, but asked, "I trust that isn't the Elluvon, sir."

"It's *an* Elluvon," Sharobi replied, and bent back to

his task, muttering, "Hand me that basin, will you? I've got something here you ought to see." He tipped his head in the general direction of the side table, and Marik retrieved the pan.

"They got the Elluvon out of the tubes," he said. "Would you happen to know where they've sent it?"

" 'They' being you," Sharobi growled. "I heard." He dropped a grey-green, nondescript organ into the basin with a pair of forceps. It made a sandy, scratchy sound. "And yes, I know where it is. It's in ICU-9, where it belongs; and for your information, Priyam, it is moribund despite our best efforts to save it." He gestured with the forceps. "Get your gloves on and take a look at that. I think we've found the causative organism, the parasite that's killing them off."

Marik suited up quickly but found it more difficult to get a glove over the hand that had been crushed in the tube case hatch. He finally squeezed it into a glove two sizes bigger than the one on his left hand. The organ Sharobi had given him to study was an interesting one: grey-green in color, it was pocked over its entire surface with regular indentations perhaps 0.5 mm. in diameter; and Marik, upon probing with a needle, was astonished to find tiny, multifilamented, flowerlike creatures extruding from them. As he watched, several of the violet-colored polyps extruded, waved their tentacles feebly, and withdrew. Two of them withered perceptibly and lay outside their cases, apparently dead.

Marik made a longitudinal incision through the body of the organ, cutting easily through the crunchy-soft tissue, and laid open the two halves of a thin, hollow, nondifferentiated sac lined with a vitreous gel. Attached to the right half, and partially buried in the gel, lay the first Elluvon fetus Marik had ever seen.

It was an exquisite little thing, about the size of his fist, compactly folded except for one of its legs, which was partially extended. There appeared to be six of them, assuming bilateral symmetry, and he could see a well-developed brain and nervous system—accounted for by numerous ganglia that were attached in sequence to each other and to the brain proper—which showed deep coral through the semitransparent blue chitin that was to be the baby's exoskeleton. It had the huge, multifaceted eyes, dark red in the fetus; but unlike the adult Elluvon, there were only one pair, placed on a horizontal line on the front of the face. A predator, then, Marik thought, and found four nares and what probably was a mouth below the eyes. In some ways, the Elluvon infant was much like an unborn human baby, and it summoned up thoughts of Mishli and his own baby, whom he had never known. Raintree Street, Kles had said. Raintree Street. He thrust the thought away and wiped his forehead with the back of his wrist to keep from contaminating his gloves. He continued his examination. The soft body was flexed and showed signs of abdominal segments, each with its own large ganglion—but then, there was that damnable cranial development and large forebrain! He snicked impatience between tongue and teeth. *Quel!* It was going to be difficult to resolve. There were no wings, nor any sign of the adult Elluvon's overlapping scutes— He stopped and probed with his needle at a suspicious bit of tissue, but it turned out to be only a shred of some kind. He blinked his burning eyes, wiped them on his arm. The main thing about the infant, the thing that bothered him most, was that it was dead. Completely, unmistakably dead. It was so perfect, so detailed, almost artificial in its exquisite perfection, with that transparent, colored milk-glass quality possessed by all developing flesh; he wondered, as he always did, whether they would have been able to save it if they had started resuscitation on the dead parent sooner, or done an emergency C-section.

Marik had a theory, and it was shared by his entire people, that every newborn, every conceptus, had a message for the world it was born into, a Word to give. He wondered what this child's Word would have been; and within himself, in a secret place where no one could watch, or scoff, or reason, he mourned the loss of this child's personality and Word, which was its alone in the universe to give.

"Priyam," he said, and was startled to see Sharobi standing by as if he had been watching for some time. "Did you know this one was pregnant?" He read Sharobi's expression correctly and narrowed his eyes in disbelief. *"All* of them?" Sharobi nodded heavily.

"All of them. In different stages of gestation. Looks like *these* damned things"—he stabbed at the flowerlike

116

coral polyps that were slowly dying in the pan—"these *parasites!*—were slowly absorbing the internal organs of the mother, exhaling the waste products as free hydrogen; they hadn't started to work on the baby yet, but it's my guess that it's just a matter of time. This is the oldest pregnancy we've found, so far." He glanced at Marik suspiciously. "What's the matter? I struck a nerve?"

"N-no, sir, it's nothing. Just something that occurred to me. Please—go on."

"I was going to point out the agglomeration of parasitic polyps around what must have been the uterus. You can see here that it's completely obscured. This stuff killed the mother; the baby was next. It undoubtedly died of suffocation when the mother went under." He squinted at Marik. "You don't believe a word I've been saying, do you?" he demanded irascibly, and Marik met his eyes soberly.

"I'm not sure, sir," he said slowly. "Look—will you give me the dead fetuses for one hour only? I want to do a comparative study."

"You've got a theory," Sharobi grinned sourly, and Marik nodded.

"Maybe I have, sir. But it's so unorthodox that I—" Sharobi lifted a hand, turning his head away to avoid the impact of the idea.

"Don't tell me about it! It's your patient!—up there in ICU-9. You botch it—and it's your hide that gets tacked up, not mine. I've got better things to do than rummaging around in those monsters!"

Marik grinned. "Name one," he challenged, but Sharobi refused to be baited. He shrugged out of his lab coat, hunched into his tunic, peered one last time into the grey-green shell where the dead infant lay, and wheeled on Marik.

"You can study the infants as long as you like, your brilliance; but you be sure—you be damned sure!—you take frozen sections when you're finished. Every medical museum in the galaxy'll be wanting tissue samples from those beings."

"Yes, sir," Marik agreed quickly. "Now—where will I find those cadavers?" Sharobi jerked a thumb over his shoulder at the refrigerated storage compartments. "Number thirty-five." He hesitated in the doorway, and Marik paused, his lifted brows a question.

"I don't suppose," Sharobi commented, clearing his throat, "that you'd want me to look in on your patient. See how it's doing."

"It you would, sir," Marik replied. "I'd be very grateful."

Sharobi nodded jerkily and left. He feels very tense about this, Marik thought, and it occurred to him that for the first time Mykar Sharobi himself might find his career in jeopardy. He frowned. If it were in his power, he could not let it happen. He owed his life to Sharobi, a long-standing debt. Also, Sharobi, like Marik, was one of the nine Priyamli left in the galaxy. It was a special calling, rather in the nature of a brotherhood, and demanded loyalties of its own. He had to help Sharobi if he could.

But first, he had to help the Elluvon. He carefully collected the two remaining Elluvon fetuses, holding each in the palm of one hand. Each was as unbelievable in its exquisite delicacy as the first had been, and each gleamed with the unfinished gelatinous shine of the unborn. He laid them carefully on the table beside the other, which he dissected out of the polyp shell, and noted absently that the smallest had a shimmering layer of frost across its head and abdomen, like a sparkling dust.

Three Words, he thought, three Words that would never be said. He wondered what they would have been. He thought of Mishli, then, with a squeezing of his hearts, and of her Word, the one Word that would say what her entire focus had been, the one Word that would be the tally and sum of her existence.

It came to him after a moment, and he smiled. All alone there in the morgue, with only the three dead alien babies to see him, he smiled, and a tear ran down his cheek and into his smile, and another hit the smallest baby and melted the frost.

Mishli's Word, of course, was Life.

Chapter VII

Neal Anderson sat on a rolling stool, elbows on his knees, chin on his fist, his unlit pipe clamped between clenched teeth, glumly regarding the only immovable object in what had just this morning been an Elluvon isolation ward. Even now, medics were dismantling the portable sections of Isolon, peeling off the seals in great flexible loops and stuffing them down the disposal chute with any micro-organisms they might have imbedded in their virtually impervious surfaces; and Morrison, suitably gowned and masked, and shielded by a screen of four Isolon panels, was spraying a potent virucide on every surface of the cot, tables, and other paraphernalia they had used for their extragalactic patient. The lab was being cleaned, every instrument Marik had used was in the autoclave, or had been, and even his culture plates had been beamed, *in toto*, over to the *Hope*. The entire sickbay was a storm of bustling activity, at the center of which, un-moved, sat Neal Anderson, staring balefully at the gelatinous mass the Elluvon had deposited in the middle of the sickbay's deck.

Although, to be fair, Anderson had to admit that it

was no longer truly a gel. It had changed somehow, developed what appeared to be a pale grey-green coating, or tegument, that was warm to the touch and neither rubbed off on the hand nor left any imprint of it. It was as if a stone could be alive: warm and flexible, but with a resilience, a toughness, inherent in its very definition. He shook his head wearily. He had been sitting here staring at it all afternoon, since he and the medics, and after a while even the ordinary crewmen, had bent or broken everything they tried in an effort to remove it from dead center of the sickbay deck. Touched gently, it yielded; struck, it was rigid and impervious. He shook his head again. He could not understand it. He wished Marik were here. If anyone could figure out what was going on, Marik was your man.

Heartened by that thought and feeling that he could always rationalize his calling by inquiring as to the Elluvon's good health (after all, he *was Skipjack*'s ranking medical officer), he got up, made his way to the wall com in the corridor—someone was disinfecting the one in the sickbay—and rang *Hope,* for Marik.

Marik was thinking about the sea. Ever since this afternoon when he had heard the diaphanous music in the tubes, reminding him of the rapture of the deep, the thought of coral had been bothering him. He was sure the coral-like polyps in the bodies of the dead Elluvon (Elluvons? Elluvonli?) reinforced the image, but he did not know why, and that bothered him. There was something locked away in his head, some fact, or facts that, applied to the Elluvon riddle, would solve a whole raft of problems, but he did not know what they were, or how they applied.

He probed at the little cadavers on the table in front of him. There was a clue here, something he was missing. It had to do with the three fetuses, and more specifically, with the middle fetus.

There were no polyps.

Why?

There were no polyps, and there should have been, for that's what was killing them off, mother and child, but this fetus was dead—of what? Perhaps it died of toxins created by the invader of its mother's body, but

120

that did not explain its own immunity. And if it were immune to the invader, why not to its toxic effects?

He examined the infants again. Internally, they were almost identical. The oldest and largest fetus had more of a superficial external resemblance to the adult Elluvon, but internally it was exactly alike both the smaller ones—with the one glaring exception of its polyps: they were present in the largest fetus—and in the smallest—but the middle child had none. Marik shook his head. It sounded like a nursery rhyme, like the old stories told by the *amah* a lost long childhood ago. But the middle one had none.

Not funny when you were talking about a malignant invader that ate its victims alive, their children with them.

He pulled the cadaver Sharobi had been working on, grabbed the boom of the recorder, and dictated into the notebook as he worked.

"Dao Marik, examining Elluvon cadaver number one, note hour, this date. Begin:

"Physically, the subject most resembles an Erthlik trilobite in appearance, with biramous limbs and setae absent, and the noticeable presence of overlapping scutes, several of which are differentiated to an unknown purpose near the posterior. Refer to input from U.S.S. *Skipjack*, this date. For convenience sake, we will arbitrarily divide the cadaver into head, thorax, and abdominal segments, although no such distinction actually exists.

"Internally, the subject possesses a large, symmetrical, bilobed central brain, with a system of evenly disseminated ganglia serving the combined function of spinal cord and medulla, neither of which is present. The digestive system is conspicuously absent, with only vestigial internal organs indicating that there has been one at some time earlier in the subject's evolutionary ascent. There is no indication, at the present time, regarding how the subject sustains itself, by way of food, drink, or the like.

"The circulatory system is more closely related to the *Arachnoidea* than to the insect. The heart consists of a slender muscular tube, probably contractile, that is placed dorsally along the abdomen, and there is evidence of aortas having extended anteriorly from it to service the

121

brain, eyes, auditory opening, and any organs that may already have been destroyed; and posteriorly to service the respiratory system and what little of a reproductive system" [part of an ovary, he believed] "can still be seen under the all-encompassing mantle of the same flowered polyps.

"The agglomeration of polyps are heavily vascularized by deteriorating arteries, and the amoebalike corpuscles float freely in the gel, which may be the subject's normal viscera or a result of its infestation. Microscopic studies show that the polyps actually devour the corpuscles, passing the waste products back to them as free hydrogen"—he paused—"see Chemical Study number fourteen," he added, and resumed, "which is collected in an expandable bladder posterior to the fringed opening in the head." As he spoke, Marik leaned over and absently pressed the swollen bladder in question, and the cadaver emitted a harmonious hum through its delicatedly frilled cleft, and rose half a meter off the slab, scutes vibrating busily. He jerked his hand back like a scalded cat and sprang to his feet, laughing almost immediately at the situation and his own reaction to it, although, he thought, he could be forgiven his surprise; it was not every day that a cadaver floated up off a slab humming at you.

The Elluvon cadaver had hit the slab again with a heavy thump. Of course. No more harmonics, no more flying. It was the same with bees, and mosquitoes, he thought he recalled, although they were Erthlik creatures, and he was not too sure about them. He would have to check. At least he knew, now, what the scutes were for: they were a means of locomotion, and a good guess that they were a means of communication, too. Perhaps the height an Elluvon flew had something to say about what sort of personality it had; you could never tell. At least he had something to go on now. At least he *knew*.

He recorded the episode and its explanation as he saw it and went back to the Elluvon infants. It was there he saw the first real difference.

His previous examination had been without prior knowledge of the adult's anatomy; now he could see the metamorphosis. The infants had embryonic gonads, well-developed circulatory systems, extending even into the shreds of tissue that he now understood would one day be scutes, and even tiny manipulators around the mouth. The *mouth,* idiot, he told himself impatiently, the mouth you saw and passed over half an hour ago! He must be more fatigued than he had imagined to miss a clue like that. He glanced at his ticket. He had missed both lunch and *dies,* the sublunch of the Einai, whose quick metabolism required smaller, more frequent amounts of high-protein food than did an Erthlik's slower chemistry. Not much wonder he had been jumpy.

So the fetus had a circulatory system, and the parent had none. Because the invader had consumed it, or because the fetus was giving him a clue he could not understand? And what of the digestive setup?

There seemed to be only one answer to that—a piece of the puzzle was missing, an integral part that fit between unborn infant and adult? In any other being, the answer was obvious: the child, the adolescent. But in the Elluvon? In the Elluvon, what?

The wall com bonged, and Marik answered, without having to touch it, "Marik. Morgue." He probed at the polyps thoughtfully.

"Dao? Neal Anderson here. How're you making out? They told me you came out of the fight on top, eh? Again?" He chuckled.

The fight? Marik thought. Was that only today? "Yes," he replied. "Yes, I'm all right. What can I do for you, Doctor?"

"It's this damned muck in the middle of sickbay. We can't work with it here, and we sure as hell can't get it up. It won't come, and that's the truth. We've tried everything but a sledgehammer, and Kopicek's bringing one up now. I was wondering if maybe you had a solution."

"A ten-normal solution," Marik murmured absently, peering close to the polyps, "of hydrochloric acid, I should think. What does it take to clear up a gel?" He fervently wished Anderson would let him get back to work.

"That's the trouble," Anderson expostulated. "It's not a gel anymore! It looks like a lump of sea coral, and you can't pry it—"

But Marik was on his feet. "It what?" he demanded of the wall com. "What did you say?"

"I said, 'You can't pry it up with a crowbar,'" Anderson's voice answered in puzzlement, and Marik shook his head impatiently.

"No, not that. About the coral." Ideas were linking together in his head, forming new patterns.

"I said it looks like a lump of coral. It does, too. Why? What's all the excitement?"

"Will you describe it for me?" he asked, trying to keep the eagerness out of his voice. "In detail, if you please." He pulled the recorder boom over toward the wall com where it would be sure to pick up every syllable.

"Fine," Anderson said. "It's, ah—about twenty by twenty-five centimeters—you know that, Marik, you found it yourself!"

"Neal. Please, if you would."

"Oh, hell. And it's grey-green, sort of, and it's pocked all over the surface, like granite, in a way, and it's hard. It used to give when you touched it, but no more. It's like hard coral, but it looks like granite. And I think it's porous to some extent."

"Why so?"

"Because I could swear I saw a couple of little flowers growing out of it—but they died off. And nobody'll believe me."

Marik stretched and laughed aloud, exultantly, locking his hands over his head and regarding the adult cadaver like a recumbent antagonist. "I believe you, Neal," he grinned. "I believe every word."

"I don't believe you," Anderson said. "What do you mean, 'You believe me'? Why should you believe me? That's crazy! Maybe *I'm* crazy. Did that ever occur to you? Maybe I've cracked up!"

"I doubt it," Marik informed him soberly. "But—now, listen, Neal, this is important: No one is to come near that object until I give the word! Is that clear? No one is to hit it, touch it, approach it until I say so. All right?"

"Okay, but—why? Is it dangerous? Poison or something?"

"No," Marik said quietly. "It's an egg."

It was a strange feeling, Paul Riker thought, to be relieved of command during an emergency and to find your ship in the hands of another officer. He could not get used to it. Even a good officer, and Simon MBenga

124

certainly was, became an intruder, an interloper, in the relationship between *Skipjack* and himself. It was like coming home and finding your executive officer sleeping with your wife. The idea of court-martial did not bother him; he could handle that when and if the time came. But the feeling of being cut off, of not being in control, was oppressive and frustrated him. The intermittent bumping of the dragons against the hull did not help; it set his nerves on edge.

For the first hour after being relieved, Riker paced his quarters, mentally rehashing his conversation with Hastings and filling in the blanks with trenchant comments that delineated his position so clearly that—had he said them—would have convinced Hastings that his course of action was unforgivable and unmilitary: but he always came back to the same end, and that was that *Skipjack* belonged to someone else now, because he was unwilling to sacrifice one man for the good of the galaxy; now he was sacrificing command of the *Skipjack* for a much lesser cause—that of Rear Admiral Hastings' poor judgment.

After a while he gave it up because it was getting him nowhere, and he had been around Marik long enough to pick up one of the alien's better habits: When faced with an insoluble problem, go around it. Take the example of water, the Einai had remarked once, which solves the problem of rocks by going around them. When Riker had laughed at Marik's contention that water was the stronger of the two, the Einai asked him when he had last seen rock wear away water.

Riker wondered how Marik's philosophy would deal with Hastings and then put the thought away from him. He knew. Marik would go around, of course, and take care of those things it was in his power to alter.

Like the dragons.

For hours now, the ships had been battered by the now-solid now-insubstantial dragon herd, and the blows, not to mention the sympathetic vibrations set up in the structure of the ship, were threatening to break both vessels apart. There had to be something he could do about it.

Water going around a rock. Dragons going around the ship. He did not like the way that came out. All right, then. How do you solve a dragon?

You could not kill them because they were someone

else's article of faith, and he respected that, and even if he did not, the man whose faith it was had the fastest, biggest ship in the fleet and was known as the Blue Death. You didn't want to cross up the Blue Death if you could help it. Scratch killing the dragons, for the time being, at least.

You could evade them, go around, as it were, which had been his first idea; but it seemed that the energy given off by your passage would send them into a frenzy from which there could be no escape but a sudden and unprovided death. Not so good. Cross off evading them. Cross off sudden and unprovided death, too, he hoped.

What else, then? What was left? And then it came to him.

You could draw them off. Bait them. Lure them away.

It was worth the try.

He made his way down to the power deck, the lift moving slowly as though power were being drained off in some manner, privately grateful that MBenga had made it clear he was not confined to quarters, and found Chief Engineer Hayashi plotting warp math. He looked up curiously and got to his feet.

"Captain. What are you——" He broke off, remembering himself, and before Riker could answer him, they were shaken by a severe impact, and Riker put out a hand to steady himself against the roll of the ship.

"Mister Hayashi," he said without preamble, "I want you to help me devise a bait."

"Bait, sir?" They braced themselves against another jolt, and Riker nodded impressively, only once.

"Dragon bait," he said. "I have an idea."

Hayashi's black eyes gleamed. "I'm with you, Captain," he said.

Marik had just finished taking the last of the frozen sections when the com gonged again. "Marik. Morgue," he said, carrying the last bits of tissue to freezer compartments, where they would be stored until planetfall and then, according to ancient Einai tradition, they would be buried in hallowed ground. There was no answer from the com, and he repeated, "Marik. Morgue."

"Marik!" The raspy voice was unmistakable, and unmistakably upset. "This's Sharobi, ICU 9. You'd better get up here."

"Coming." Marik slammed the freezer shut, make quick work of his scrub, and tossed his lab coat in the nearest receptacle. When Sharobi sounded loud and irritable, there was not much to worry about; when he was quietly upset, it was hysteria time. He ran.

The nurse outside ICU 9 handed him a sterile gown and mask as he entered, and he "washed" his hands under a bank of select radiation similar to that used in Transport to decontaminate personnel and cargo coming aboard from strange and exotic planets or plague ships. Mostly the planets; there really were not many plague ships prowling around the galaxy, he reminded himself wryly. He elbowed the stud snapping off the scrub lights and entered the Intensive Care Unit where Elluvon—the Elluvon he had rescued—lay dying.

There were other humanoids in the room; he could see them only visually, on the edge of his consciousness, but what struck him first, and hardest, was the haze of fear in the room. Of panicky, unthinking fear. It fairly stank with it. He closed his mind with an effort and saw Sharobi coming toward him. Beyond, over the older man's head, he saw the sensors connected to the MAX, indicating extreme agitation on the part of his patient. Its physical responses, those which registered at all, were extremely weak and unsteady. Sharobi was treating it—by removing the polyps! No wonder it had panicked!

He crossed to the MAX and pushed back the plastex hood, heedless of the gust of methane gas that swam out into the unit, unseen, odorless, and deadly, and palpated not only the being's belly, as before, but its head, too. Sharobi and the two nurses on duty watched wordlessly as he precussed abdomen and thorax and palpated the head again, and then again, the belly. One of the nurses, a junior, made a grimace and turned her head away as his fingers sank deep into the being's soft tissue, but the Elluvon gave no indication of tenderness; indeed, it was as if there was no sensation at all.

Marik's face gave no inkling into what he might be thinking. There was nothing, Sharobi mused irascibly, more impassive than an Einai when he wanted to look impassive. Now Marik had gone beyond mere impassivity

127

—he looked absolutely blank. That was a certain sign that Marik was on to something; what irritated Sharobi was that he could not figure out what it was. And he was not about to ask.

Marik measured the being's head and for the first time frowned a bit and closed the MAX hood, his eyes narrowed thoughtfully.

"Well?" Sharobi demanded, in spite of himself. Marik looked at him as though seeing him for the first time.

"Let's get it into OR 1, stat," he said crisply, and Sharobi nodded sharply at the nurses, very pleased. Now we would see some action. Marik had spent a great deal of time—close to a *suspicious* amount of time—in his research, but now he was going to take some positive action to save his patient. Good. Good! He had been almost disappointed in the boy, but now, by thunder, we would see some of that brilliant technique he was known for!

"Mind if I assist you, Priyam?" he offered gruffly, and Marik, his slit pupils dilating with the intensity of some hidden emotion, although his tone was one of sincere regret and respect, answered quietly, "I'm counting on it, sir."

Only later did Sharobi understand the reason for his concern.

The facility known as OR 1 was a surgeon's dream. Completely enclosed in its own transparent capsule—which was large enough to accommodate a MAX, and did, during surgery—it had only four stations: surgeon and surgical assistant, which stations were serviced by ample glove boxes; surgical nurse's station, which was a console to the left of the surgeon and controlled the gross motion of most of the instruments, which were attached to flexible, extensible shafts fixed into the overhead, and could rotate a full 360 degrees in any direction; and lastly, at the assistant's right, the anesthetist's station, which also controlled heart/lung and other specialized devices, including the cryogenic equipment.

Retractors, hemostats, and other such instruments were customarily held by robot devices, which never wriggled, itched, tired, or became the least bit shaky, even after several hours' sustained effort.

There was also a mirrored backdrop to prevent the

surgeon's becoming lost when and if his sphere of endeavor extended around to the patient's blind side and a flip-up screen that magnified the surgical field to a panorama and improved conditions to the extent that risky procedures once considered "watchmaking" became commonplace by reason of the magnifying screen and computer-augmented fine-motion instruments.

It was to this facility, then, that Marik brought the Elluvon; it was in this capsular surgery that he secured it, MAX hood open, capsule aerated with the Elluvon's own special air mix, properly sterilized and balanced. Sharobi wondered why he seemed so grim.

Alexander Meng, the chief resident in Anesthesiology, met them at the OR, saying that his boss sent regrets but was tied up in conferences and couldn't make it; and Sharobi, who knew him to be an unremitting bigot, resolved to replace him—probably with Meng—at the earliest opportunity. He caught Marik glancing at his ticket, and he checked his own.

"Meng," he snapped impatiently, "find out what's keeping McKeon, will you?" But before he reached the wall com, Carol McKeon arrived. She was a pretty thing, an earthling with short red curls that defied the current style and an air of competence that belied her youth.

"Sorry I'm late," she apologized. "Are we all here?"

"No." Sharobi wheeled on Marik even as he said it. "No—not exactly. But we should be soon." He had that fey look again.

"You have a procedure to start, Priyam," Sharobi reminded him bluntly. "Let's leave the cryptic comments until afterward." He started toward the scrub room, Meng and McKeon moving uncertainly after him, and Marik surprised them all by what he said next.

"I don't intend to operate on the Elluvon, sir," he said. "I never did."

Sharobi stopped where he stood and said, without turning, "You *what?*"

"If we remove those polyps, Priyam," Marik explained humbly, "it dies! According to my findings—"

Sharobi made an unprintable suggestion about Marik's findings and finished heatedly. "You may stand by if you like, Priyam, and take findings until you're blue in the face! But I intend to give that patient all the help I can!"

"I—think—not!—sir!" There was no more humility in Marik's voice now, and while he spoke quietly, there was no question about who was in charge here. "The surgery has gone into complete stasis, as of"—he checked his ticket again, and Sharobi realized, with a sinking feeling at the pit of his stomach, why he had been keeping such careful watch of the time—"two minutes, forty seconds ago. I wrote the software for it myself. We remain in stasis for one hour.

"You needn't try that, Doctor Meng," he added, as the anesthesiologist tried the door unobtrusively and then openly tugged at it. "I warned Security not to let us out until I gave the signal. We're on Isolation Alert."

Sharobi's heart sank. Isolation Alert was the term commonly used when some virulent organism escaped the confines of a lab or unit, and under that code not only the Isolation unit involved but the two next outer units were shut off. The central unit was fogged with bacteriocidal detergents and virucides, then sprayed with superheated steam, and the outermost unit was subjected to as near a true vacuum as it was possible to achieve outside of space itself.

Marik had done a thorough job, he thought. They were trapped here until the Einai chose to set them free. By that time, he reflected sickly, the Elluvon would have gone out, and the galaxy, as an incidental sidelight, would be at the mercy of those bobbing blue globes that everyone was getting so excited over. But the Elluvon—the patient, the individual—that was the important thing. Alive—it had the right to live! It was their job to help it live.

Sharobi walked over to the plastex-encapsulated operating theater and looked at the Elluvon lying there, its many-faceted eyes glazed and dull, its scutes standing up slightly, like a dog's hackles, as if it were being inflated from the inside. Those damned polyps, he thought, growing, multiplying, eating this being alive, and—damn Marik! —her surgeon refused to help her. He could not fathom it. Marik, like the Shimshenli, like all Priyamli, was consecrated to Life. This was so unlike him! What was he getting at, what was he trying to do? He turned, smouldering.

"So we're just going to stand around here while you
130

let your patient die, is that it?" he demanded of Marik, and the Einai shook his head.

"You know better than that, sir. I didn't come here to let the Elluvon die." He went to a cabinet in the scrub room and brought out one of the tablets the medical students used for sketching during surgery and a stylus. He lay them on a nearby stool and went to the wall com to request a printout of the notes he had taken throughout his research into the nature of the Elluvon.

"Do you mean to say," Sharobi demanded, in his measured sarcastic monotone, "that you actually expect me—to sit down—and read through a bunch of dry scientific treatises while your patient expires through sheer neglect?"

"You may do as you like about that, sir," Marik retorted crisply, "but I'll tell you this: If you don't read them, you've got a nasty surprise coming to you in about an hour or so!" He tossed the printout down in close proximity to his chief, picked up the pad and stylus, and settled himself against one of the braces at the surgeon's/ surgical assistant's station, which permitted a comfortable half-standing, half-seated posture and afforded him a full view of his patient as he worked.

He gazed at the Elluvon through the plastex and was gratified to see that—if you took his theory into account —things were going along nicely. The tegument was peeled back in a half a dozen places, revealing small nubbins of coral-like outgrowth, and the head seemed strangely wrinkled and collapsed, in marked contrast to the continued slow swelling of the body. Something strange was happening, and he thought he knew what it was. Predictably—again, going along with his theory—the Elluvon's brain was still shrinking, just as he had noticed aboard *Skipjack*, and would continue to shrink down to nothing, just as the other adolescent organs had, until they were used up by—

He shook his head. He dared not think so far ahead, hardly dared even to hope. But if it were true, he thought, fighting down his excitement, if what his findings led him incontrovertibly to believe—

He sketched a globe on the corner of his pad, surrounding it lazily with another, and another, and another—

"We saw them on the screen," McKeon said softly, and

he knew that she had been sitting there quietly for some time, watching him draw. He made no reply, but began shading in the first one, making it a globe in the true sense of the word, giving it dimension and form.

"They all speak so well of you," she ventured, and shrugged. "It seems funny just to sit here, you know?" Her tentative smile asked for friendship, and he pulled a wry smile, quickly gone.

"It feels funny to me, too, if that's any help," he offered. "I don't like this any better than he does." He tipped his head toward the stool where Sharobi, stiff and uncommunicative, had reluctantly picked up Marik's notes and begun to read them.

"Then why don't you do something!" she burst out in an urgent whisper, and he regarded her with such cool detachment that she looked away and muttered, "I'm sorry. It's just"—she shook her head and faced him, her eyes swimming with angry tears—"I think you're trying to *make* it die!" Marik studied her face sadly for a long moment before he spoke, and she flushed under his candid scrutiny.

"No," he said gently, as to a small child, "I'm trying to make it live! See here"—he turned the notebook to a clean new sheet—"let me draw you a picture—and maybe you'll understand what I'm trying to do."

She leaned forward curiously to watch him, while outside the dragons pounded the hull with their vast tonnages of innocence, threatening to split the ship asunder.

The *Skipjack* saw it first. The lookouts, diligently watching their monitors, had seen nothing for hours but the dragons, space, and the hard pinpoint brilliance of the stars; then the starboard watch came alert as a mere fleck, a dark mote, swam easily onto her screen and grew there like an alien culture. She rang the bridge and the combat information center simultaneously.

"Bogey off the starboard beam," she warned, and heard the ship sound general quarters. Because she was already at her station, she resumed her watch as the Krail battle cruiser grew to life-size on her viewer and wondered idly what the captain would be thinking, right about now.

The captain, down in Engineering, was delighted. He

held the metal sphere in both his hands and beamed at Shigeru Hayashi over it as if he could read some strange and wonderful fortune in its smoothly polished surface.

"This is what I was looking for, Mister Hayashi. This is just what I wanted." He wet his lip in that preoccupied manner of his and said, "You're sure you can pack enough charge in this to attract a dragon?"

To which Hayashi replied confidently, "Captain, I can pack enough electricity in that thing to attract the whole damn' herd."

Riker weighed the sphere in his hand, wondering at its heaviness, and said, "Yeah, I guess you can at that. The only thing that troubles me is, once we've rigged it, what do we attach it to? What do we put it on that'll draw those dragons far enough off for us to get away?"

The alarm bells rang general quarters, and the wall com piped. Hayashi got it. "Power deck. Hayashi." He gestured. "For you, Captain." Riker crossed to the com, while crewmen hurried past.

"Riker."

"MBenga here, Captain. I thought you'd better know we have company. The Krail battle cruiser *Mactau* is standing dead off our starboard quarter, just out of range of our guns."

"Has she made signal?"

"No, Paul. Nothing. No signal, but still, no belligerent moves, either. I think she probably wants the Elluvon, but not bad enough to face the dragons to get it." A light began to glimmer pleasantly in Riker's imagination, and he turned the sphere in his hand and viewed it from every side.

"Think they're afraid of the dragons, eh?" He smiled at the faceless com.

"Aren't you?" MBenga's metallic voice asked dryly, and Riker's smile grew and grew. Even Hayashi joined in now, getting the captain's drift and going along with it. He gave Riker both thumbs up.

"Not anymore, my man," Riker told the com, "not anymore." He rang off and weighed the sphere happily in his hand, thinking of the enormous expanse of electrically neutral metal the *Mactau*'s hull presented, and how easily a charged metal sphere—call it bait—could be planted against it by one man.

Provided it was the right man.

Say, an officer with a bit of background in science, a sense of adventure, and a little extra time on his hands.

Say, himself.

He kissed the sphere jubilantly—and grinned.

"Bonanza!" he exulted.

Chapter VIII

Mykar Sharobi finished reading the last page of the printout and with a long-drawn-out exhalation put it down slowly. He looked up at Marik with an expression of disbelieving wonder and deliberately got to his feet.

"*Quell!*" he muttered. "That's—quite a body of work. Quite a theory." Marik paused in his final few lines of sketching and said, "There's more to it than that—and you know it!"

Sharobi hunched his massive shoulders and fixed his dark, brooding gaze on the Elluvon, who was now virtually covered with the grey-green polyps. Every so often a flower would extrude and wave its petals—tentacles—delicately, and Sharobi repressed a shudder.

"Why didn't you let me in on it?" he asked pensively. "Whether you're right or not—it's a heavy load to carry by yourself."

Because if I'm wrong, I don't want the roof to fall in on both of us, he wanted to say. Because if I'm wrong, you're the man who'll have to bring charges against me, and I want it to be as painless as possible. And if I'm right—what better man to have here to witness this wonder that the Elluvon must be? But he only said, "I've done a sketch of the intermediate stage. I think it'll fill in the gaps in my report."

Sharobi took the drawing pad and saw four individual figures: First, an egg, a simple grey-green ovoid pockmarked like granite; a double sketch of the larval stage, drawn directly from the little infants in the morgue, with functional mouths, eyes, legs, hearts, and digestive systems. Marik had used a green pencil to indicate the polyps, which were present only in the female and were grouped loosely around the larva's embryonic ovary, which contained a single undeveloped egg. The male larva was devoid of polyps, slightly larger, and—male.

The fourth drawing was that of the Elluvon in the MAX, but it was labeled "adolescent stage" and was devoid of digestive system, legs, and most of the circulatory system, although the amoebalike corpuscles floated freely through the gel that replaced the previous stage's viscera. It had reached sexual maturation, however, and the developed egg was seen surrounded by a wall of polyps, as if it were a shell gland. It was obvious from the sketch—and from the information in Marik's report—that the polyps drew upon the body's protoplasm to build the developing fetus. In this case, the child feeding on the mother's body was a literal fact; it devoured her.

"But the Elluvon's stopped breathing," Sharobi protested. "And even if that thing in *Skipjack*'s sickbay *is* an egg—you'll notice I said *if*—then why didn't the polyps stop proliferating? They've eaten her alive! And for what? She's already delivered! Why do they keep it up? It doesn't make sense!"

For the first time in a long time, Marik smiled. "She's not dead yet," he said, taking the sketch pad back. He began to draw the last picture. "If I'm right, there's another stage to go."

Sharobi was spared answering him by the sound of a hum, faint at first, then rising in volume, though not in pitch, until it took all the attention. Meng and McKeon hurried to the surgery capsule and breathed against the plastex as they watched, half fascinated, half in horror, the strange transformation that was taking place in the Elluvon. Small objects around the room started vibrating in a kind of a sympathetic reaction, and Sharobi stared unbelievingly, eyes narrowed, jaw stubbornly set, as a tiny fissure appeared in the dorsal aspect of Elluvon's encrustation. The hum continued, fluctuating slightly in pitch from time to time, and it was a full minute before they realized that it was a subtle music, cracking the shell.

"Metamorphosis," Marik said quietly from where he stood.

The fissure widened, and through it, slowly at first and then more confidently, came what appeared to be a blue mist, a smoky presence, a bobbing blue globe. Marik shut his eyes, smiled gratefully to himself—and closed the sketchbook.

"This is the fourth stage of the Elluvon," he told them. "The true adult. Insubstantial, intelligent, telepathic. The accumulated gaseous wastes—like the carbon dioxide in our lungs—is exhaled at the proper pitch to crack the husk. I suspect that is the way the young larvae emerge from their eggs and the adolescent from the larval cocoons."

As he spoke, the globe moved agitatedly about the capsule, seeming to examine it minutely from the inside. Then, as Sharobi and the others watched open-mouthed, it passed unchecked through the capsule wall, touched each of their heads for a brief instant: Sharobi stood fast, although tense; McKeon made a little shriek and squeezed her eyes shut as if she were standing under a cold shower; the globe had to float all the way across the room to touch Meng, who had chosen that moment to try the doors again and came to rest on Marik's forehead, where it expanded and settled slowly, enveloping his entire head in a blue halo. Marik stood very still while this was going on, and Carol McKeon was crying silently, both hands over her mouth. Meng had said nothing, done nothing. Judging from his expression, Sharobi thought, it was unlikely that he would for a while.

"You are the being Dao Marik?" asked a soft and distinctly feminine voice gently, retreating with the mist and reforming into the shape of a young humanoid girl, standing a meter above the deck in front of Marik. She seemed uncomfortable in this form and kept twisting her hands in front her like an anxious ghost.

"I am," Marik answered evenly. "And you are the being Elluvon."

"No," she corrected shyly, "*we* are the Elluvon; *I* am the being Muse." And then quickly, eagerly, softly, "Are you pleased with the gift?"

"The gift." Marik hoped his voice was noncommittal. "Oh—oh, yes, the gift." He looked for help at Sharobi, who shrugged complacently. There was the sense of laughter in the room, from Muse.

"The 'egg,' " Muse explained. "The child. What greater gift than this, my own child?" In his secret heart, Marik knew disappointment.

"You must understand"— Marik chose his words carefully—"that we are unfamiliar with your species, Muse; we would be unable to care for the child. We appreciate your gift, but—" The mist blossomed around his head again, paused and became Muse once more. Her smile was a music of its own. "You don't understand," she said soberly.

"Until a child is born," she told him, "it is irrevocably tied to the past; it is the embodiment not only of its parents, but in some part, the genetic embodiment of every ancestor. Therefore, it is not only linked to the past—it *is* the past.

"In the same way, the unborn child is the future: of the parents, of the forebears who live through the child, and of the ancient ancestors, long dead. Therefore, the child *is* the future, linked irrevocably to it by reason of its existence. And while you have a child, Dao Marik, you, too, are linked to the past—and the future.

"This, then, is the Elluvon gift: the unborn child, link with the past and gate to the future. As long as it remains unhatched, your ship may travel up and down what you call '*time*' at will. Once it hatches, however, you must return to your own time within one solar day—the time it takes the infant to emerge—or be forever trapped WhenEver you are." She took what would have been a deep breath in a substantial being and smiled girlishly. "I'm glad *that's* over," she confided. "I was afraid I'd forget what to say."

"Time travel?" Meng asked blankly. "Did she say 'time travel'?"

"I would give my right arm," Sharobi breathed, "to go with them."

"Oh," Muse continued in a subdued tone, "I wanted

to thank you for what you did, trying to rescue me from the tubes and taking care of me—and everything." She appeared to be growing smaller and less and less humanoid. "It was awfully nice of you."

"It's my responsibility to do those things," Marik told her kindly, "but I'm glad it pleased you. You're very welcome."

She had become a ball of blue light hovering at his shoulder. "Oh," whispered the voice to the still room, "there's one more thing."

"Yes?" The misty globe approached his ear and bobbed there shyly.

"I like you—a lot—even if you *are* just a humanoid."

In evident high amusement, Marik murmured, "Thankyouverymuch," and flushed a bit.

"Oh, for God's sake," Sharobi growled in disgust, turning on his heel and starting for the door. Meng beat him to it and found, to his surprise, that it opened at last. The incurably romantic Miss McKeon responded to Muse's naïveté by clasping her hands together and asking Sharobi if that was not the sweetest thing he ever saw.

"No," Sharobi retorted with offended astonishment. "No, it isn't!" He seemed embarrassed that anyone would ask. "Now that you ask, no!" He wheeled on Marik as if for help, but instead ventured irascibly, "I suppose you will have no objection to my informing Captain Kris and Captain Riker about this unexpected turn of events, Priyam, so that they can relay the information to ComFleet?"

Marik made an expansive gesture, the blue globe still hovering at shoulder level, and with a great deal of self-satisfaction said, "Be my guest, sir." Sharobi almost expected him to lick cream off his whiskers. Or canary feathers.

"I've been your guest, dammit, for over an hour now! And I don't care to repeat the procedure! Although," he relented a bit, "you made a very lucky guess about the, uh"—he gestured awkwardly at the globe—"the lady, the Elluvon, Muse, whatever you call it."

"Muse," offered the disembodied voice distinctly, and Sharobi pulled one of his infrequent and surprisingly appealing grins.

"Muse," he corrected himself, and then, rather hopefully, "I don't suppose you'll be able to be with us for very long. Damned shame. But we'll muddle along—"

"Oh, yes!" The blue globe bounced gaily a few times in midair. "I will be with you ever so long. I am to study your species as my contribution to our shared knowledge. It is to be my lifework." Sharobi missed a step and stumbled, clearing his throat. He blinked rapidly a few times and forced a sour smile.

"Welcome aboard," he said, "I suppose."

And back in the OR 1, inside the capsule, what was left of the Elluvon's—Muse's—chrysalis lay forgotten, an elongated grey-green mound, like an abandoned tomb, covered with violet flowers.

Kles Mennon stood behind the helm, his thin, bald lieutenant—the man called Ilai—piloting the *Tsai*. They were headed away from the rendezvous of the Federation ships, away from *Mactau*, escaping the pull of her tractor beams. Win hild-Sar stood beside the pirate captain, saying nothing, his colorless eyes, like his colorless face, expressionless, watching his ship recede on the viewer.

"We leave you here," Mennon said pleasantly. "We are still within transport range and yet beyond the capabilities of your formidable armament. A nice compromise, don't you think?"

Hild-Sar, who had visions of collecting the reward money on Mennon's head, pursed his lips and lifted his brows. "If you insist upon avoiding us, Master Mennon, how can we deliver your prisoner to you? Marik, I believe you said?"

"Ah, well." Mennon shrugged and smiled his charming smile, but his eyes were cold as a snake's at the mention of Marik's name. "I manage to be available when I'm needed, my friend. You get me Marik, and I'll be there to collect him!" He gestured courteously toward the transporter grids, and hild-Sar stepped reluctantly on one of them.

"How will we know where to contact you?" One last, desperate stab at it. Mennon smiled again coldly, showing all his teeth.

"I'll be around, my friend," he reassured him, even as the switches were depressed. "Have no fear—you'll be seeing me again!"

140

A glimmer and he was gone, and hild-Sar stepped down from the spacious grids aboard his own vessel, annoyed at having failed to capture the elusive Kles Mennon. He ignored the salutes of two guards at the portal and took the lift to the bridge.

The two Federation vessels were displayed on a viewing screen that diagrammed everything, and he found himself looking at a diagram of *Skipjack* hard by a diagram of *Hope*, with diagrams of the cavorting dragons moving between and around them. Several of his officers leaped to their feet and saluted him, but he made no response.

"Get me the captain of the *Skipjack*," he ordered. He kept his eyes on the screen. If it were not for the dragons, he reflected, how easily they could take both the unarmed *Hope* and the smaller *Skipjack*! What fortunes in drugs and slaves could be his, to bring back triumphantly to the imperator! But the dragons—

He shuddered involuntarily. The light flashed on his com, and he answered it. Simultaneously, an image of an Erthlik, massive, black, and self-possessed, appeared on the screen. Hild-Sar cleared his throat.

"I am Commander Win hild-Sar, commanding His Majesty's ship *Mactau*." He waited pointedly.

"Simon MBenga, temporarily in command of the U.S.S. *Skipjack*," the black man said quietly. "What can I do for you, Commander?"

Hild-Sar smiled, showing long, blue-white teeth. "Ah, yes," he ventured, "it seems that you have in your possession a certain animal, a certain *being*, that is the property of His Majesty. We would like to make arrangements to permit you to return it at once."

MBenga's face did not change. "I'm afraid I don't know what you're talking about, sir."

Hild-Sar leaned forward on both hands, bracing them against the austere, tablelike console that was his helm. "What I am talking about"—he dealt his words flatly —"is a being called an *Elluvon*, which your ship kidnaped from neutral space while on its way to the Imperium! We know that you have it! It has been seen aboard your vessel by eyewitnesses! And I insist you return it to us immediately or face the consequences." He straightened slowly and awaited the results of his candid threat, but

141

if he expected a reaction from Simon MBenga, he was to be disappointed.

MBenga sat there motionless for perhaps ten slow seconds and then asked calmly, "Is that the end of your message, Commander?"

"It is!"

The screen went dead, and hild-Sar realized with well-controlled fury that MBenga had rung off. There was no message, no confirmation or denial, not even a response to his gauntlet. Merely a blank screen. Unthinkable. These animals had no sense of propriety. Had not even the intelligence to realize how easily the *Mactau* could—would!—crush them, once the dragons were past. Well—they would know. They would know soon enough what it was to wear a shock collar around their necks. He would see how mannerly this MBenga could be then.

When they captured both ships.

When the dragons passed.

The dragons were the whole problem, and it was not a question of these particular dragons themselves but of the dragons of Ets-la. The dragons, which were featured in Krailim's nightmares and stalked her most ancient history. The Krail's only natural predator, the Ets-la dragon was as ancient an enemy to the people of that planet as the serpent was to the Erthlikli. Even back in the old, benighted days, when Krail still believed in a deity, the spirit of evil had been depicted not as a serpent but as a dragon—the dragon of Ets-la. The legends had been expunged, the religious murdered, centuries ago. The fear remained. They drank it with their mothers' milk and dreamed it on stormy nights. It was the one racial weakness they acknowledged, and they guarded it jealously, lest someone else find out.

Hild-Sar wanted the slaves aboard the *Skipjack* and the *Hope,* and he wanted the glory. But the dragons! He repressed a shudder. They would wait until the dragons left. They would have to wait.

They were ready to set the bait. It had taken them a long time to set up, but the problems had been many and trying. It was one thing to postulate a bait crammed with a negative charge, and it was possible to make one, using the ship's Van de Graaff accelerator; but then you had to put it into something to shield it, so you wasted time hunting up a Faraday cage, and could not find one, and ended up having to rig one out of spit and baling wire, or, more correctly, a metal box lined with teflon. Then there was the question of the timing device, so that Riker could be well out of the way when the bait was sprung. They had to be careful of it: Set too late, and a crewman from the *Mactau* could conceivably blast it off the hull; too soon, and it would discharge into *Skipjack*'s hull, which, incidentally, had built up a powerful positive charge from those damned dragons brushing up against it, picking up electrons with their big positive bodies, all day. Either way, they would lose the bait—and, undoubtedly, Riker into the bargain.

By the time they had gotten that far, Hayashi was sweating over the timer, and Riker was struggling into a suit, two techs helping him with the umbilicals and bakpak. As he fastened them, Riker noticed for the first time in all the years he had climbed in and out of them, that his suit's fittings were made of metal. He felt a twinge of frank apprehension. With the powerful forces he would be dealing with, a bit of badly placed metal could spell the difference between life and death. When the bottom dropped out of that Faraday cage, there was going to be a powerful jolt—unless anyone nearby was well insulated. Even then, he thought grimly, even then—

"What about these fittings, Mister Hayashi?" The Japanese examined them and made a self-deprecating chuckle. Hayashi always laughed when he was ill at ease or embarrassed. Riker would have felt a lot more comfortable if the affable Oriental had remained serious.

"Well—you will probably have enough insulation with the suit," he hedged, "because it's lined with rubber—and of course, the air space inside will give you some protection, too. And then, you will be a good distance away when it arcs. I'm not worried," he finished with another chuckle. He wiped his upper lip with the palm of his hand. Riker picked up the heavy cage and turned to Hayashi soberly.

"I am," he said, confidentially, "but not very much." He started toward the cargo hatch, where the two techs were waiting for him, and they ran through a final check of his meager equipment: belt chargers, for thrust; a pulse

143

weapon, set on +5; a container of epoxy, to attach the box to the *Mactau;* a communicator ("Just in case, sir") even though he had insisted on strict radio silence. Just those few articles. Someone rechecked his bakpak. His helmet. Hayashi came over in that rolling seaman's walk of his, wearing a concerned expression.

"Sir, you don't have to do this, you know. If you want to think it over, one of us could—" Riker grinned and shook his head.

"Not a chance, Mister Hayashi." He pushed the stud that shut the airlock, and there was the sound of the pumps. They could see only the back of his helmet and his bakpak as the outer hatch opened and Paul Riker stepped off the edge of the *Skipjack* into the stars.

It did not look far on the screens, or big. A perfect picture, a few orderly centimeters, and you would be gone from *Skipjack* to the *Mactau.* In practice, there was a considerable difference.

First, there were the stars; not stars like you saw from a planetary surface, the same familiar stars ticktocking around in the same familiar patterns, season in and season out; the north star and the Dippers and the Three Kings in Orion's belt. These stars knew no up or down, no spring or autumn; these stars stayed right where they were, and it was man who tumbled headlong into their static fireworks, lost in the argent rain of them. The Krail ship lay far ahead on a horizontal plane to his position, but a mere inclination to one side or the other could topple him so that *Mactau* would appear to be standing on its nose; and if he looked away without knowing where to look back to, he could get permanently lost. If not for the *Skipjack,* he thought with satisfying practicality, with reasonable logic. If not for the monitor screens that kept him in their view, the sensors that sniffed out the morsel of human flesh among the icy brittleness of the stars and marked him as human, and therefore belonging to the ship. He only hoped *Mactau's* sensors would miss him for a while longer.

For that was the danger; that was the mortal jeopardy. When *Mactau's* sensors picked him up, their electron beams—equivalent to small-arms fire—would lock onto the nearest heat source, in this case, himself, and pick him off neatly. He hoped the suit would insulate his body

144

heat from their scanners. He hoped the bait would work. He hoped he would get back alive.

The Krail ship was getting noticeably larger, awesomely larger, with greater visual detail as he moved closer, when a *something* whisked past him at tremendous speed, seeming slower than it was because of its mammoth proportions. Riker felt the hair standing up on the back of his neck.

A dragon.

From the ship, they could not be distinguished from pale clouds of distant dust, from ghosts on the sensors, from echoes audible only to the sensitive electronic ear. Out here they were gigantic wraiths, enormous phantoms, like the great, humping memories of whales long since disappeared. He half turned and saw several more of the beasts sporting nearby in a kind of witless curiosity about this spacesuited pygmy in their midst. He noticed that they were avoiding the ships, seemingly by instinct, perhaps by necessity, and then he reminded himself that both ships had developed a strong positive charge.

Like charges repeal, said the didactic voice of Miss Stanhope, his second-grade teacher, from a classroom in the back of his mind. Repel, Miss Stanhope, he corrected. She never could pronounce it properly, but then, her major had been sociology, not English. Back in those days, *everyone's* major had been sociology. A few people could even spell it.

Thank God, he thought, for the Fordham Project, which set things to rights again.

A second dragon brushed by him, much too close, and another and another. Riker frowned and took a closer grip on the Faraday cage. Could they sense the bait, he wondered, and then discarded that notion. If they could smell that bait, he would have been inundated and electrocuted, all in one fell swoop, before he could put words to it. No. It wasn't the bait they wanted.

Himself, then? Could they sense the electrical neutrality of him, realize somehow that anything not actively positive had to have some negative balancing quality, no matter how small? Not likely, he thought, but he drew his pulser, anyway. By now he should have been through the herd, past the spectral dragons and their very real buffeting, for he was nearing the Krail ship in earnest. He supposed the dragons were avoiding the positively charged ships rather than actually following him. They wouldn't be likely to follow him, he thought. Why would they be interested in him?

A big transparent hulk came at him suddenly; he fired at it reflexively and was astounded when the pulser kicked like an elephant gun and threw him into a wild tumble in the general direction of the Krail ship. His arm felt as if it had been torn off at the shoulder.

Oh, hell, he thought, it's that *like charge* repelling *like charge* again. He righted himself with some difficulty, using his belt chargers in short bursts and sighting by *Mactau*'s running lights. He left the Faraday cage hovering while he flexed his arm thoughtfully. He had come a long way on that one bump, fast and probably unnoticed by the Krail sensors. What was a burst of positive energy against a mass of positive energy to a sensor? Less than nothing.

He glanced back at the sporting dragons, one or two of whom seemed ready for another run at him. He gauged the distance between himself and the *Mactau*. Twenty minutes, maybe, on belt chargers. Belt chargers, that showed up on sensors. Maybe, just maybe, the dragons' bulk would mask his use of the pulser. It was worth the try.

He waited for the next curious hulk that blossomed transparently against the stars, making them shimmer like jewels under running water, and fired, the force of it speeding him on his way. He had been smart this time, had fired from the belly, so that his body absorbed the greatest kick at roughly his center of gravity and spared him the dizzying gyration that was so awkward to control. He fired again at a sounding behemoth and again was abruptly shot toward his goal. He felt a little like a hockey puck, but he was making good time. He didn't suppose it mattered much to a puck; a few more healthy impacts like that last one, he thought ruefully, and he wouldn't be in any shape to care, either. But for now, he was getting there, faster than he had ever supposed he could.

The Krail lookout saw what the sensors might have missed: There were intermittent short bursts of positive energy where there should have been no energy, where— he reran all the information he had with mnemonic precision, gratified once again that the race called the Krail were favored with inhumanly precise memories and total recall—where there should have been only the barest fluctuation when the dragons sported. The Krail knew a great deal about the dragons. The list of offworld scientists they had killed to ensure themselves of the facts was impressively long and prestigious. There could be no mistake. Something was amiss.

He signaled the bridge. "Suspicious energy off the port quarter, Commander," he announced quietly. They never shouted. It was a matter of pride with them that they never raised their voices, even in battle.

There was the orderly haste of the ship going to general quarters, during which not a man spoke, not a sound was made. Weapons banks were armed, silently. Electron beams were made ready. Sensors tasted space and saw that it was good.

It was too much to ask, Riker told himself, that the charge in his pulser would last forever. Even as he fired again at a lone beast who had no intention of rejoining the herd, just yet, he felt the pulser grow warm in his hand. There was very little counterthrust, which meant that the charge was just about gone. Just as soon make use of the last of it, he thought, and winding up, pitched it over the plate in his best college-varsity style. Even the counterthrust of that will get me somewhere, he thought, watching it soar (like all the others should have soared, and some had) back toward his own ship.

There was an abrupt lance of light from the *Mactau*, and it picked the pulser out of existence in an instant and disappeared. Riker took a firmer grip on the Faraday cage. All right, he told himself, all right, now. They've seen you, or at least, they've seen the pulser. The heat of course, he figured quickly, they home in on the heat source. That didn't leave him much chance. Think. *Think.* They'd pick him up any minute now. The lone dragon that had been hounding him—Riker thought of him as an old bull whale—approached again, nudged him and sounded. Using his belt thrusters, Riker dived with him, keeping the formless body, force, energy, of the dragon between himself and the Krail ship. A beam of light lanced out and shattered in a silent crackle against the suddenly substantial hulk of the dragon and was gone before he could blink. The old bull, transparent as before, made a wide loop and nosed curiously closer to the Krail vessel.

Attaboy, Riker urged it silently, attaboy, old man. You take us right in there! Right down her gullet! Special delivery.

The *Mactau* loomed against the stars, dark and deadly and far, far too big. A bright white beam lanced out blindly for the merest second, and there was an instantaneous cluster of dragons at it, even as it vanished. They moved restlessly, milling and bumping each other in apparent frustration—or hunger. Could it be hunger? Riker followed the dragon eagerly as it moved closer to the Krail ship. Maintain, gentlemen, he thought at the hungry, disappointed dragons, give me five minutes, and you'll have a bellyful!

"Sir, Whitey's firing on the dragons!"

Whitey. The fleet's nickname for anything Krail.

"Go to general quarters." MBenga made a gesture, and the big forward screen leaped to life, displaying occasional star-shimmers to mark where the dragons must be and a brilliant beam of light, there and gone, from the *Mactau.*

"They're using electron beams!" Jen exclaimed, her blue ruff quivering in agitation. "Won't that attract the dragons?"

Guns shook his head slightly. "Gone too quick," he replied curtly. "Short pulse. Have to sustain it—maybe a half minute—to attract dragons."

The com piped, and MBenga thumbed the stud. "Bridge. MBenga."

"Hayashi, sir," came the agitated voice metallically. "Sir, I thought you should know. The captain's out there! With the dragons, sir."

"Say again." MBenga's fathomless black gaze turned to the depths of space and the sporting of behemoths.

"The captain," Hayashi said distinctly, "is on his way to the Krail ship—carrying bait to get the dragons off us—and onto them." MBenga shut his eyes slowly and opened them again.

"And you didn't see fit to report this to me." Cool. Quiet.

"I was under orders not to, sir," Hayashi defended uncomfortably.

"There are no orders—on this ship," MBenga replied crisply, "—but mine!" He wheeled on Jen. "Get me Mister Marik, aboard the *Hope!* And see if you can raise the captain."

"Aye, sir." Her hands flew across her board, and MBenga settled back slowly in his chair and touched his com.

"Transport sector," piped the voice.

"Stand by to beam one across, personnel."

"Unable, sir. Power's down, and our field's unstable." MBenga scowled to himself and rang off. *"Can you raise the captain,* Miss Jen?" he repeated with some asperity, and she threw him a helpless glance over her shoulder.

"Still trying, sir." MBenga sat back uneasily, drumming his fingers slowly against the arm of his chair, hoping against hope that the *Mactau* would not get smart and go to laser weapons before it was too late.

The old bull sounded again, diving down, if it could be called "down" thousands of feet and looping up again very close to *Mactau*'s bow, and Riker felt a sense of accomplishment that he was able to keep up as well as he could. You really needed three hands, he thought: one for each belt charger and one for the cage. The cage, with the compressed electricity of a thousand thunderstorms locked in it, ready to flash free the moment the shielding fell away. The bull dragon was making shorter, faster runs, requiring more of his attention. They're getting hungry, he thought. They're really getting hungry.

His communicator *beeped.*

He applied thrust with both his chargers and hoped the dragon would continue its straight-line dash while he flipped open his com.

"Riker."

"Leave the bait, Paul," MBenga's voice was crisp and professional. "Get back here on the double. We'll figure another way."

Riker regarded the communicator with the same insolent grin he would have afforded MBenga himself, had he been there. "The hell you yell," he retorted, and snapped it shut. There was a bright light and a terrible jolt and at the same time an instantaneous bump from the old bull dragon, and Riker found himself waking up from a dream of falling, feeling shaken and strange. The Faraday cage was still in his hand, in a virtual death grip, and he was drifting aimlessly under the belly of the *Mactau*.

The electron beam, he thought fuzzily, that's what it was. The old bull must have turned, or sounded, or something, and they got a good clear shot at me. He found time to be grateful for his insulated suit. If not for the metal fittings, he thought, he'd probably not have felt a thing. Then again, if not for the suit, he reasoned fuzzily, he probably would have been fried to a crisp. Judging from the way he felt, he probably had.

The great metal hull plates of *Mactau*'s underbelly drifted by languidly, and he came to himself of a sudden and realized where he was and what he was supposed to be doing. My God, he thought, I'm right under the thing! It's right on top of me! I made it! I'm *here!*

Using his chargers, he got as close to the hull as he could and hooked a leg around a convenient docking stanchion. He squeezed a ring of epoxy onto the hull and filled in part of the center; then he lifted the Faraday cage up to it, floating it in gently until the lid sank into the viscous circle and stuck fast. He set the timer for three minutes, carefully brought out the key with his glove-thick fingers, and locked it into the *on* position. Now no prowling Krail crewman—or anyone else—could stop the timer from snapping the cage open and summoning the impatient herd into the sphere's electric extravagance. He checked his chronometer.

Three minutes. He had a little less than three minutes to get out of here before the firewords started. He started to put the empty tube of epoxy back into his sleeve pocket but thought better of it and tossed it away. Inadvertently, the key to the timer flew with it, the whang slipping easily off his wrist and floating away. He snatched at it, but it swam just out of his reach and kept going. Hard on the heels of *That was stupid, Riker,* came the knowledge that no one was going to be unlocking the timer, anyway. He shrugged it off and started to maneuver himself into position to push off for his own ship when he felt a twinge, a tug, at the back of his curled leg and froze motionless. He reached a careful hand down the back of his trouser

150

leg and felt the problem: His suit had snagged on some tiny projection of metal, and he was caught there, like a fish on a hook, not daring to move. One wrong move, and his suit would rip, the air would puff out in one final breath, and the late Paul Riker would float endlessly down the corridors of space, drifting among the asteroids.

That didn't sound so hot. He didn't like it. He checked his chronometer. Two minutes, ten seconds left. He tried straightening the leg a bit and felt the threads catch more strongly. He bent it back. No joy there, either. He looked at the Faraday cage, ticking away without a sound. He thought about his leg. He thought about the asteroids.

There was one other way he could get out, but it would take courage he wasn't sure he had. A man could tighten the built-in constriction bands, say, around his thigh, pull himself free and hightail it for the ship. He could probably make it without losing his air, he figured, but it was almost sure to lose the leg. The leg, and the commission, and the whole way of life. Worst of all would be losing the *Skipjack*. He could stand the thought of losing the leg, but giving up the *Skipjack* would kill him as surely as the open cage would. The cage. He checked his chronometer again.

One minute, forty seconds.

Decision time, he told himself, and he started to tighten the constriction bands even as his mind protested that he would rather stay and die than give up *Skipjack*. When it was painfully tight, he took a deep breath, fixed his sights on *Skipjack*, and tore free. The air blew like a balloon, out of just a little rip, and he loosened the fabric of his suit from the stanchion with its sharp projection—nothing much, just a couple of millimeters of rough steel someone had not bothered to pare down. His leg was very cold, bitterly cold, but he could breathe. He'd make it, he thought. He'd for damn sure make it.

He pushed off *hard*, assisting himself with his belt chargers and mentally flinching from the lances of electron beams that could, at any minute, knock him from here to there and give him a nasty jolt. But before he was in range, he saw the tumbling, sporting stupidity of the herd and felt a warmth for it and a kinship. He could feel his leg swelling, and there seemed to be insects crawling all thing through the suit. It had been such a *little* rip.

A brilliant beam of light hit one of the cavorting dragons, turning it visible for just an instant before it—obviously—died, and Riker recognized it as the friendly old bull that had seen him safely to the *Mactau*. He turned and cursed the Krail then; he did not know why except that the dragon had been such a harmless oaf, and his leg hurt so badly, and he was going to end up losing the *Skipjack* and the leg—

The light was fantastic. Riker had placed the cage well, and the cage must have dropped exactly on time, for the sphere was radiating dancing bands of blue electricity in 360 degrees of arc, and the dragons were upon it instantly, crowding, devouring, battering the *Mactau*'s hull until it actually shifted in space, while all the time, scintillating sparks and bolts of electricity flickered across their insubstantial bodies and shot through their glimmering movements. Spangles of electricity flared and twinkled on their hulks.

It was more than Riker could believe, this neon parade of dragons, this spectacle of blue—fire—glittering, these thousand thousand resplendent lights dazzling his eyes and glimmering against the blackness of space. Even as he wondered at the lights, holding his leg with both hands as he plummeted back toward his ship, the insects on them seemed to become wasps, sparkling, incandescent wasps, that stung his leg beyond all feeling and left him to fall into a black well of unconsciousness.

When he woke, Riker was lying in an open MAX, and Marik and MBenga were there with him. Hovering over Marik's shoulder was one of the bobbing blue globes that had given him such a fright this morning. Had it only been this morning? Memory flooded back, and he reached for his leg, trying to sit up. A wave of dizziness hit him, and he let Marik push him back onto the pillow.

"My leg?" he asked tiredly, and the alien smiled.

"Still there. You chose the right ship for rendezvous, Captain. *Hope* has some very fine facilities." There were bandages.

"That's another one I owe you," Riker told him. He could not understand why he was so tired. He focused on MBenga. *"Mactau?"*

The black man laughed his fine laugh. "Long gone," he

said, "with those dragons chasing after her like a pack of hounds. That hild-Sar has got more trouble than he knows what to do with right about now." He nodded at Riker for a time and said softly, "You did a fine job of work there, Paul. You certainly did."

Riker closed his eyes and smiled. "Hell, yes," he said. He must have dozed for a minute, but then he opened his eyes and looked at them again.

"Didn't we all."

Epilog

Both the U.S.S. *Skipjack* and the starcruiser U.S.S. *Hope* departed rendezvous at the designated time, bound for drydock on Eisernon, where they put in for repairs. Officers and men were given a thirty-day leave.

Captain Donelang Kris requested and received permission to visit the galactic museum of music on Monastary, to continue his research into the nature of music.

Captain Paul Riker, U.S.S. *Skipjack*, fully reinstated after an informal hearing at which not only his own officers and men, but Priyam Mykar Sharobi, of the U.S.S. *Hope*, testified, elected to spend his leave visiting the pavilion of his science officer, Lieutenant Commander Dao Marik.

The being Muse, of the race called the Elluvon, rejoined her gestalt briefly for the intergalactic ceremonies held at Federation Central, promising to return before the next star run.

Ensign Parry Kaplan began a crusade to Save the Dragons, which was swiftly quelched by the ambassador to Xholemeache, who had trouble enough as it was. Kaplan responded by getting up a petition to have him replaced. There is no word on the outcome of that petition as yet.

And lastly, the messenger who brought Riker and Marik their orders at Marik's palatial pavilion overlooking the Single Sea, told them rumor had it that Win hild-Sar, commander of His Imperial Majesty's battle cruiser *Mactau*, had been summarily replaced. There was no word of his fate, nor of the name of his successor.

The orders the messenger had left were sealed, not to be opened until *Skipjack* was under way; but there was a faint imprint on the packet, an impression made by a stylus, regarding this ship, these men.

Riker held the packet up to the light, slanting it so that the firelight fell across its vellum surface and made readable shadows of the print.

It carried one phrase, and one phrase alone:

Code name: Timeslide.

Half a Million Hardcovers in Print

Over Eight Months on
The New York Times
Bestseller List

Charles Berlitz
The Bermuda Triangle

THE
NATIONWIDE
#1
BESTSELLER!

The Bermuda Triangle book
that will continue to astound the world
long after the others have "disappeared!"

COMPLETE WITH PHOTOS, MAPS, CHARTS, AND DRAWINGS

SUPERIOR
FANTASY AND SCIENCE FICTION
FROM AVON BOOKS

NEW W#6RLDS

THE TABOO-
BREAKING ANNUAL
COLLECTION OF
NEW SPECULATIVE
FICTION

EDITED BY
CHARLES PLATT
AND
HILARY BAILEY

In the tradition of NEW WORLDS #5—
twenty four more vivid, thought provok-
ing, totally original visions by brilliant
young writers whose ideas herald the
future of science fiction—and of mankind.